Glitch Mitchell
and the
Unseen Planet

Also by Philip Harris

Novellas

The Girl in the City

Short Stories

Bottled Lightning

Curfew

Saviour

Only Friends

Glitch Mitchell and the Unseen Planet

Philip Harris

Glitch Mitchell and the Unseen Planet
by Philip Harris

ISBN 978-0-9938887-6-2

10 9 8 7 6 5 4 3 2 1

Cover design by M.S. Corley

Editing provided by:
Red Adept Editing Services
Clio Editing Services

Formatting by Polgarus Studio

For Buster, Jean
and Frank

Contents

Introduction

When I was growing up, one of the highlights of the summer and Christmas school holidays was the BBC's children's programming. Every morning they'd air a Tarzan movie and episodes of the old black-and-white fiction serials from the 1930s—*Zorro*, *The Lone Ranger*, and *Buck Rogers*. I enjoyed them all, but my favorite was *Flash Gordon* starring Larry "Buster" Crabbe.

I'd eagerly sit down each morning to see how Flash, Dale, and Doc managed to get out of whatever mess they'd got themselves into the day before. I don't know how many times I watched each series (I remember them being shown every year for most of my childhood, although I doubt that's actually true), but they stuck with me, and I've always had a soft spot in my geeky heart for those serials (helped by the 1980 movie, of course).

The book you're about to read grew out of my love of those old serials. Originally conceived as a series of interconnected short stories intended to be posted on my blog, the idea quickly grew into the full-length novel you hold in your hands now, but I've kept the episodic format and tried to recreate the feel of those fast-paced, over-the-top, cliffhanger-driven stories that I enjoyed so much as a kid.

I hope you have as much fun reading about Glitch and his adventures on the unseen planet as I did writing them.

Philip Harris
July 2015

CHAPTER ONE
Gateway to the Stars

Five hours before Dwayne "Glitch" Mitchell died, he was standing outside a hotel, waiting for a bus and wondering if the whole "Win a Trip to NASA to See the Greatest Scientific Discovery the World Has Ever Made" thing was an elaborate practical joke. He checked his watch for the fifth time and looked down the street. A yellow bus rolled steadily toward him. A handwritten sign propped in the front window read NASA.

Glitch felt a flicker of disappointment. He'd been expecting a blue luxury coach emblazoned with the NASA logo and perhaps a painting of an intrepid spaceman or Neil Armstrong's portrait, not a battered old school bus that leaned heavily to the right. Still, he couldn't be too picky. He was visiting a secret NASA base to see an artifact that might change the world. He was just a science fiction geek. Real scientists would probably kill to be standing where he was, school bus or no school bus.

The decrepit vehicle shuddered to a halt, and the door

began opening. It hissed, rattled, and scraped, moving slowly, as though it wasn't entirely convinced it wanted to let Glitch on board.

"I take it you're Dwayne Mitchell?" said the driver, squinting at Glitch.

Glitch nodded, smiling.

The driver frowned at him. "Come on, we're late."

Glitch hurried onto the bus. Distracted by the driver's hostility, Glitch caught his foot on the edge of a step and stumbled forward. He tried to turn the trip into a run up the steps, but there were only three of them, and he just looked even more stupid. The driver sighed and asked Glitch for his ID. Glitch wrestled his driver's license out of his wallet and showed it to the driver. He ticked Glitch's name off of the list on the clipboard he was holding and closed the door.

Glitch blushed. He counted eleven more people on the bus, most of them men and most of them seated in pairs. Only a middle-aged man, who was so excited he looked in danger of wetting himself, sat alone. At the front of the bus sat a dour-faced man and a woman Glitch would never have the courage to sit next to. Both of them were wearing Air Force uniforms.

Several of the passengers frowned at Glitch as he hurried down the bus. He was the youngest person by at least five years. He was wearing black jeans, a battered old jacket, and a *Firefly* T-shirt that read "Also, I can kill you with my mind."

Anxiety wrapped its arms around Glitch, the feeling

familiar, almost welcome. He wasn't one of those people. They were nerds and geeks, just like him, but like a Trekkie at a *Star Wars* convention, Glitch was out of place. He was a different breed of geek. Sure, they put on their *Doctor Who* boxers one leg at a time just as he did, but then they put on grown-up clothes over them. Clearly a T-shirt and jeans were not appropriate attire for an exclusive trip to NASA.

Keeping his head down and trying not to trip over anything else, Glitch made his way toward the back of the bus. As he passed the uniformed woman, he glanced at her.

She smiled. "Nice shirt."

Glitch blushed again, mumbled his thanks, and continued by, picking the second-to-last row. He barely had time to throw his bag onto the seat next to his and sit down before the bus moved.

As the vehicle lurched away from the curb, the dour man at the front stood. He was tall and thin faced, in his late fifties, Glitch guessed, with gray hair. He had the imposing air of someone used to getting his own way. He pressed his lips together into a thin line as though this was the last place he wanted to be.

"Good morning," he said. His voice was gruff and tinged with more than a little contempt. "My name is Colonel Vaughn. I'm in charge of the Gateway Project."

Just hearing those words made Glitch smile.

"I'm sure I don't need to remind you of the... unusual nature of your visit today, ladies and gentlemen. You will be the first civilians, outside of NASA employees, to visit the project. I trust that you will treat this occasion with the respect it deserves. Not Twitting or Facebooking or whatever."

Glitch saw a young woman off to his left surreptitiously slip her smartphone out of sight.

Colonel Vaughn gestured toward the woman in the uniform next to him. "Now, I'm going to hand you over to Captain Anderson. She'll be showing you around, answering your questions and so on. Captain Anderson?"

Captain Anderson stood and turned to face them, her smile broad. Her face was much more welcoming than the colonel's. "Thank you, Colonel, and congratulations to all of you." She smiled again then began explaining the logistics of their visit.

Glitch tuned out most of it, paying just enough attention to get the gist of any critical instructions while he scanned his fellow contest winners. They all looked very serious—scientist types mostly, probably professors. Again he considered his T-shirt and cringed inwardly.

By the time Captain Anderson had finished talking and answered the handful of questions the passengers had, they'd arrived at the Rockies. Captain Anderson invited them to come to the front of the bus if they thought of any more questions or needed anything, and sat down.

The people around Glitch chattered away, getting to know each other and speculating on the nature of the gateway. Glitch was content to stare out the window at the dry landscape. He was almost disappointed when the bus turned down a narrow road then bounced and bumped its way through a checkpoint and into a narrow parking lot.

Captain Anderson stood, and the bus's door reluctantly opened. "If you'd like to follow me, please."

The passengers filed out of the bus, the air filled with nervous excitement. After a tall, almost emaciated man checked their IDs and marked their names off on a tablet, four serious-looking men in military police uniforms led them to the security screening area.

It took over an hour and a half for the ten civilians to shuffle through two different scanning machines, have their IDs examined, and get their hands swabbed. Their cameras, phones, watches, and anything else that might conceal some sort of recording device were taken from them for "safekeeping." They'd be returned at the end of the visit. After that, they had to stand in line while, one by one, they approached a security desk to answer half a dozen seemingly random questions about their personal circumstances.

A young man with short black hair, dressed in a sharp black suit, was in the queue in front of Glitch. There seemed to be some issue with his identification, and it had to be checked and rechecked for almost fifteen minutes before he was allowed through the checkpoint. When Glitch stepped forward for his own interrogation, he was just about ready to admit to whatever they cared to accuse him of. Glitch stumbled through the questions, convinced he was about to be thrown out or arrested. When the guard smiled at Glitch and welcomed him to NASA,

Glitch almost hugged her in relief.

After yet another ID check, they were handed clip-on plastic passes and led through a small, unassuming door into the NASA facility. They walked down a series of tunnels lit by dozens of portable halogen lamps. The walls were uneven, just rock painted white.

An older man, short and stocky with an eager grin, fell into step beside Glitch. "It's exciting, isn't it?"

"Uh huh," said Glitch.

The man offered his hand. "My name's Winston. I'm a molecular biologist."

Glitch shook the man's hand. It was warm and slightly sweaty. "I'm Glitch. Electro-mechanical engineer."

"Glitch?"

"Yes, it's a long story."

Winston raised his eyebrows, seemingly waiting for Glitch to tell his story. When he didn't, Winston shrugged. "What was your essay about?"

Glitch struggled to find a few words to describe his essay. He'd been surprised to find out he'd won. He'd thought his rambling descriptions of alien planets and creatures that the Gateway Project might uncover were self-indulgent and trite. Apparently the judges disagreed.

"I… wrote about the things we might find with the gateway."

"Like aliens?"

"Yeah…"

"Oh." Winston seemed to have been expecting something a little more erudite.

They walked for a few empty seconds until Glitch thought to ask the man about his essay. The man's face lit up, but as he opened his mouth to respond, they reached a door. This one was much bigger than the one they'd entered through, and it looked a lot more solid. In the middle of it was a broad wheel, like an airlock.

"Ladies and gentlemen," said Colonel Vaughn.

A hush fell over the group.

"Before we go onto the site, let me remind you once more that this is an active research facility operating under the watch of the United States Air Force. Try not to wander off and get shot."

A wave of nervous laughter rippled through the group, but Colonel Vaughn didn't look as though he was joking. One of the guards opened the door and ushered them inside.

The room beyond was smaller than Glitch had expected. He'd had visions of a huge hangar lined with dozens of rack-mounted computers covered in flashing lights and dials. He'd imagined row upon row of control consoles manned by NASA scientists in crisp white lab coats. A video display twice the size of a cinema screen would dominate one wall, and the gateway itself would sit on a raised platform in the middle of the room, humming and glowing with energy, eagerly waiting for mankind to unleash its potential.

Instead, he got a cave roughly the size of a basketball court. There was a single control desk, just wide enough to seat a couple of people. A few pieces of equipment lay scattered on the ground nearby. At least there were computers. A bank of them stood along one wall, complete with flashing lights and LED displays showing temperatures and short strings of digits that presumably meant something to the five people in lab coats.

Three of the cave walls had been painted white. The fourth, the one opposite the entrance, was bare rock. Embedded in the rock was a five-sided metal frame slightly larger than a standard door. It looked somewhat coffin shaped. The frame appeared to hold a flat sheet of dull silver metal. There were no markings on the metal or its frame and no door handle, but a small metal box with a bright red light on top sat on the ground nearby. A thick metal cable ran from the back of the box to the lower right-hand side of the frame.

As the visitors shuffled into the room, no one wanting to stray too close to any equipment, one of the lab-coated scientists faced the group. She was an Asian woman in her late forties, with bright, excited eyes and a soft, friendly face. Her chestnut hair was pulled back into a ponytail.

"Ah!" said the woman. "You're finally here. I was beginning to think the colonel had whisked you off to interrogation." She laughed as though she was trying to make it clear she was only joking and that the Air Force hardly ever did that sort of thing. "My name is Doctor Grace Zheng."

Glitch recognized the name. She'd been one of the competition judges. She had a distinctly upper-class English accent, each word clearly enunciated, but an underlying excitement belied her stuffy heritage.

"I'm sure you're all very keen to see the gateway in action, so I won't keep you waiting too long. I would like to congratulate you on your success in the competition. There were so many fantastic entries, it was hard to choose the winners." The doctor beamed at them for a moment as though she expected the group to break into spontaneous applause. When they didn't, she waved them toward the wall with the frame. "Well, come on, don't be shy."

The group made their way across the room, barely able to contain their excitement. Winston, the man who'd spoken to Glitch, was almost running. Glitch ended up standing next to him in the middle of the line of eager visitors, right in front of the gateway. The doctor and Colonel Vaughn were nearby, next to the control panel. As the excited guests jockeyed for position, the colonel motioned at them to step back, insisting they keep a safe, respectful distance from the gateway.

Glitch glanced over his shoulder. Captain Anderson was standing behind him. She smiled, and he gave her what he hoped was a friendly smile in return. Blushing, he hurriedly turned back to the gateway.

Doctor Zheng nodded to one of her colleagues and smiled at the impatient group. The red lamp on the box at the foot of the frame turned green. Glitch felt the hairs on his arms stand up and his chest tighten as energy filled the air. A low-pitched humming grew in intensity until he felt the ground vibrating. The smell of ozone filled the air as the humming was joined by a brief buzzing sound that repeated every few seconds, as though a train of motorcycles was racing through the room at high speed.

Zinnnn.

Zinnnn.

Zinnnn.

The sheet of metal within the frame, if that was what it was, rippled. The shifting was subtle at first, but it grew stronger. Concentric rings emanated from near the top of the frame and rolled across the metal. Another set of rings joined the first, then a third. There was a loud crack, a sharp snap, and blue-white electricity burst into life around the edges of the gateway. The energy leapt from the frame, crawling across the wall like lightning.

The scientists were glued to control panels, but no one seemed overly concerned about what was going on. Apparently, that was how the gateway worked. The electricity writhed and sparked for a couple of minutes. The room began to feel smaller, the air denser. Glitch was starting to get a headache when, with a loud pop, the gateway started to glow, pulsing gently with a silvery light.

The tendrils of energy retreated. As they vanished, the gateway stopped glowing. But where the metal had been dull and lifeless, now it was a silver mirror that rippled occasionally, as though it was a pool of mercury and someone was dropping pebbles into it. The motorcycle buzzing stopped, and the humming was barely noticeable. The oppressive atmosphere in the room faded.

The whole process couldn't have lasted more than three minutes, but it left Glitch, and the rest of the visitors, speechless.

"Ladies and gentlemen," said Doctor Zheng, "I present to you the Gateway to the Stars."

Most of the visitors burst into a round of applause. Someone shouted, "Bravo! Bravo!"

Glitch found himself grinning and clapping along. "Did she just call it a Stargate?" he said, mostly to himself.

He heard a snort of laughter behind him and turned to see Captain Anderson trying to stifle a grin. Glitch looked toward Colonel Vaughn. He was frowning at them both.

"He doesn't seem very happy," whispered Glitch.

"No," said Captain Anderson. "He doesn't approve of the competition—feels this is no place for civilians, no matter how desperate NASA is to sway public opinion in its favor."

The man beside Glitch held his hands over his mouth, his eyes wide and tears forming at their corners. NASA had certainly won over at least one of its visitors. The man in the black suit stood on the other side of Glitch, and he seemed a lot less impressed. He was standing perfectly still, his narrow eyes fixed on the gateway.

Doctor Zheng joined the group, and she was walking down the line, shaking hands and answering questions.

No, it wasn't dangerous as long as you stayed at least six feet away. Yes, they had sent and retrieved probes, but she couldn't discuss their findings at this stage. No, they hadn't sent a human being through it. Yet. And no, they didn't need any volunteers.

Colonel Vaughn trailed behind her, still bristling with

resentment.

The tearful man was much more effusive, and it took Doctor Zheng several minutes to extricate her hand from his grip and answer his series of ever more technical questions. Eventually, she managed to shut him up by promising they'd have more time to talk later. Glitch wanted to ask the doctor a question, something smart, but when she appeared in front of him, his mind went blank. He just smiled, carefully shook her hand, and congratulated her.

She moved on to the man in the black suit. Doctor Zheng reached out a hand, a broad smile on her face.

"Congratulations," he said, not taking her hand. "You must be very proud."

The doctor lowered her hand, her smile wavering slightly. "Thank you, I am, but it has been a real team effort."

When the man didn't say anything else, she stepped past him toward a young woman whose excitement was tangible; she danced from one foot to the other as though she couldn't quite believe she was there. Or she needed the bathroom. Doctor Zheng had just turned to talk to her when the man in the black suit lunged forward, swung his arm around her neck, and dragged her backward toward the gateway. Glitch didn't see where the gun came from, but it was small, probably easy to hide, and it looked as if it was made from beige plastic rather than metal.

The man pressed its barrel against the side of the doctor's head and looked around the room. "Everyone stay where you are, or our friend Doctor Zheng won't be making any more scientific breakthroughs."

Glitch felt Captain Anderson lightly touch his back, and he stepped sideways, out of her way.

She moved forward, arms outstretched, palms raised. "Okay, don't do anything rash. Whatever it is you want, we can work it out."

The man in the suit gave a little snort but didn't reply. He just kept pulling Doctor Zheng toward the gateway.

"Don't be a fool," said Colonel Vaughn. "There's nowhere for you to go."

The man in the suit stopped and stared at the colonel, a puzzled look on his face. "Of course there is, Colonel."

It took Glitch a couple of seconds to realize what the man meant, but Anderson was quicker. "No one has gone through the gateway," she said. "We don't know what's on the other side."

The man in the black suit smiled and shook his head slowly. "We both know that's a lie." He lowered his gun and fired three shots at the box at the base of the gateway.

"No!" screamed Doctor Zheng.

She struggled in his grip, trying to free herself, but the man's arm was locked around her neck. The gun clicked, either jammed or empty, and the man threw it away.

Colonel Vaughn barked orders, and the four guards raised their guns, but they were too late. The man in the black suit grabbed the doctor with both arms and propelled them both through the gateway. A loud hissing, like a burst of static, filled the air for a couple of seconds then rapidly faded to nothing, and they were gone.

The humming from the gateway grew louder again, rising in pitch. Its mercurial surface shuddered and bulged, distorting its reflection of the world like a funhouse mirror. Captain Anderson ran toward the gateway.

"Get these damn civilians out of here," shouted the colonel, fighting to make himself heard above the steadily increasing noise from the gateway.

Most of the visitors had taken cover when the firing started; now they ran toward the exit. They gladly followed the military police's commands, happy someone was taking charge of the situation.

Glitch crouched on the floor, doing his best to present a small target for any stray bullets. He watched the captain run toward the gateway and launch herself through it. There was another burst of static, louder and rougher than the first.

"Come on," shouted one of the guards.

Glitch turned and ran toward the exit. He was the last person left in the room—even the guards were standing on the other side of the door. For a terrifying moment, Glitch thought they were going to lock him inside to contain whatever explosion was about to go off.

He was almost at the door, ten feet away at most, when the room gave a sickening lurch. The walls elongated, pulling away from him until he felt as though he was looking down the inside of a straw. The doorway shrank, the guards seemingly being dragged down the straw. Glitch was still running as hard as he could, but the door just got farther and farther away. One of the guards reached out, his arm stretching to comical lengths and the tips of his fingers just inches away.

In desperation, Glitch lunged toward the outstretched hand, but he felt himself stop and hang in mid-air. Then the world snapped back. The doorway and the guards rushed toward him, returning to their normal proportions. But Glitch was traveling backward toward the gateway. He clutched desperately at the control desk, but his hand skipped across the smooth metal.

Seconds later, Glitch hit the gateway.

A deafening wave of static crashed over him. The copper tang of blood filled his mouth, and he felt something warm and wet trickle from his ears.

A vise closed around Glitch's chest, crushing the air from his lungs, and his heart stopped.

CHAPTER TWO
Returned from Death

Somewhere deep within the Colorado Rockies, NASA has discovered a gateway to another world. Thanks to his contest-winning essay, Dwayne "Glitch" Mitchell is one of the few civilians who gets to see it. But as the head of the project, Doctor Zheng, proudly discusses the gateway with the contest winners, an armed man takes her hostage. The man damages the gateway and flees through it, pursued by Air Force Captain Anderson. As the gateway implodes, Glitch makes a break for the exit, but he's caught by the device and dragged backward toward the gateway.

Glitch clutched desperately at the control desk, his hand skipping across the smooth metal. Seconds later, he hit the gateway, and a deafening wave of static crashed over him. Blood filled his mouth, thick and coppery, and he felt something warm trickle from his ears.

Iron bands wrapped around Glitch's chest, forcing the air from his lungs. His heart stopped.

Eons passed.

Light burst behind Glitch's eyes. His muscles contracted until they were so tight, he thought they might snap, then they relaxed. Energy flooded his system, and his senses fired into overdrive. He was cold, so cold, and he was suffocating. He opened his mouth and dragged a long, deep breath into his empty lungs. His chest felt as if a thousand needles had been hammered into it. He tasted blood.

Someone rolled him onto his side. The floor beneath his head was hard and gritty, and he smelled dust. He coughed and spat, trying to get the taste of blood from his mouth.

"Dwayne? Are you okay?" It was a woman's voice.

Glitch tried to speak, but the effort triggered another coughing fit.

"It's okay, take it easy."

The someone pressed their hand against his throat. His heart was racing, although the pain in his chest had eased off.

"Open your eyes."

Glitch tried to obey, but his eyes were stuck together, frozen. Panic gripped him, and he began to push himself upright. Hands pressed him back down.

"Don't worry. I'm going to put some water on your eyes, Dwayne. Okay?"

Glitch nodded, fighting down the panic and another

coughing fit. Lukewarm water splashed against his eyes and ran down his face.

"Try now."

Glitch flinched as he forced his eyelids apart. The light was blinding. Glitch squeezed his eyes almost closed again and peered at the shape bending over him. It was definitely a woman, and he had a feeling he recognized her face. He felt her name scuttling around in the back of his mind, just out of reach.

"My name is Captain Anderson. Do you remember me?"

Glitch frowned in concentration. Her name sounded familiar. He knew it from somewhere but couldn't quite nail down where.

"We met at the Air Force base. You were visiting the gateway."

Memories clicked into place. The competition. The trip to NASA. The man in the black suit. The explosion. Glitch raised his hand to shield his eyes from the brightness. He couldn't see much, but the ground around him was red rock.

"Dwayne, we need to get behind some cover. Can you sit up?"

Glitch's arms and legs ached and the needles in his chest were still there, but otherwise he felt okay. He nodded.

"Good, we lost you for a while there." Captain Anderson helped Glitch sit up and handed him a metal water bottle. "Drink some of this, slowly."

As Glitch sipped the water, he looked around. They weren't at NASA anymore. At least, not at the site where he'd been a few minutes ago. They were in a small cave. The walls were an orange-red rock that looked a bit like sandstone. The ground was dirt, packed hard by the passage of time or feet. Four sets of lamps, each one barely more than a halogen bulb stuck on a metal pole, sat around the cave. A gateway similar to the one Glitch had come through was embedded in the wall. Its surface was dull and gray. The cave had only one exit, a narrow corridor opposite the gateway, just wide enough for them to get through. Stacked next to the exit were four large black cases.

"Where are we?" asked Glitch.

Anderson glanced toward the exit. "Can you move?"

Glitch nodded, the movement setting the world spinning around him. With more help from Captain Anderson than he would have liked, Glitch stood. He let Anderson guide him across the cave. When they reached the black cases, she helped him sit again. After making sure he wasn't about to pass out, Anderson stood and went through the cases.

Glitch looked at the gateway. It was virtually identical to the one at the other site, maybe a bit bigger. Three brown rectangular packs were attached to the wall around it. They looked like parcels. A small red flashing light sat on top of each one. Glitch closed his eyes. The needles in his chest were fading. He took a few deep breaths. The air was dry, stale.

Anderson knelt beside him. "Here."

Glitch opened his eyes again to find Anderson offering him some tablets.

"They're just painkillers," she said.

Glitch thanked her and took them, washing them down with more of the water. There was a beep from somewhere across the cave, and Glitch looked at the boxes attached to the gateway. He couldn't be sure, but it looked as if the red lights were flashing more quickly. "Captain? Are those bombs?"

"Yes, but—" Cursing, Anderson sprinted across the cave.

She'd made it halfway there when the first explosive detonated and scattered shards of rock across the room. Glitch rolled over, covering his head with his hands, just as the second pack of explosives blew.

A wave of red dust billowed across the cavern, cutting visibility. Chunks of rock rained down on Glitch, and he flinched. A few seconds later, there was another explosion and the sound of tearing metal. A lump of rock about the size of his head bounced past Glitch and shattered against a nearby wall. A slightly smaller rock caught him on the shoulder, and he swore.

Glitch lay on the ground for a moment, waiting for more explosions, until curiosity got the better of him. He raised his head. Anderson was barely visible through a thick cloud of red dust. She lay sprawled on the floor a few feet away from the gateway. She wasn't moving.

The gateway was badly damaged. Half of it had been

torn from the rock wall, and the bottom right corner was bent outward. The gray surface was gone, and the rock that had been behind it was blackened and smooth. Thin lines ran through it as though it had been subjected to great heat and had melted and solidified dozens of times. The explosions had left ragged indentations in the wall, and chunks of rock were scattered across the ground. Glitch rubbed his shoulder, grateful he'd escaped the worst of it.

Trying not to worry about the ringing in his ears, Glitch stood and staggered across the room. His legs felt slow and unresponsive, and he stumbled a couple of times on the uneven, debris-scattered floor. Glitch knelt beside Anderson. A thin trickle of blood ran down the side of her head from a cut above her eye, and she was covered in a fine layer of dust, but she was breathing.

He touched her shoulder. "Captain Anderson?"

Anderson's eyes flickered open, and she flinched; whether at the brightness of the halogen lamps or the pain, Glitch wasn't sure.

"Ouch," said Anderson.

Glitch frowned then realized it'd been a joke. "Are you okay?"

"I think so. What about you?"

"Yeah, I'm fine."

"Good. Help me up."

Glitch stood and held out his hand. He waited, his hand in mid-air, while Captain Anderson carefully moved her arms and legs. Then she grabbed Glitch's hand and pulled herself upright. Anderson closed her eyes and staggered sideways. Glitch stepped forward, ready to at least try to catch her if she fell. She didn't.

Anderson stood still for a few seconds, her breathing slow and deep, then opened her eyes and smiled. "Thank you, Dwayne."

Glitch grimaced. "Please don't call me that. Only my mom and dad call me the D word. Everyone else calls me Glitch."

"Glitch it is, then."

"Thank you, Captain."

"My name's Scarlett. We may be here awhile, so I think we can dispense with the formalities."

"Scarlett as in O'Hara or Johansson?"

"Johansson, definitely."

"Okay… Scarlett as in Johansson. If you don't mind, I'd really like to go home now."

Anderson looked at the twisted remains of the gateway. "Well, you can't go that way, and I need to find Doctor Zheng. So for the time being, you're stuck here with me."

Glitch looked around the cavern. "And where exactly is *here?*"

"Honestly? We think it's another planet, but other than that, we don't know."

"But you've been here before," he said, gesturing toward the boxes.

Anderson hesitated, and Glitch raised his eyebrows.

"Yes. We sent a team through two days ago."

"And they never returned?"

Anderson frowned. "No… they spent ten minutes here, assessing the situation, and came back. We've been preparing for a full expedition since then. Yesterday, we brought through the first of the supplies. That's what the boxes are."

"So why did Doctor Zheng lie about sending people through?"

"The colonel. He wants to keep things as quiet as possible. Says he doesn't want all those 'damn reporters' poking around at all hours of the day and night."

"So who's the guy in the black suit? He seemed to know the truth."

Anderson shrugged. "According to his entry, his name is John Smith."

Glitch gave a little laugh. "John Smith? Didn't you guys do a background check or ask the NSA about us or something?"

Anderson glared at him. "Of course. Everyone was checked out—even you, Dwayne. How did your John Constantine costume go down at Comic-Con last year, by the way?"

Glitch blushed. "Right, sorry. Errr… so how do we find Doctor Zheng? Don't you guys all have some sort of tracking device? For emergencies?"

Anderson tapped her forearm. "Like a radiographic subdermal implant?"

"Whoa, you have that?"

Anderson laughed. "No, this isn't a TV show. There's only one way out of this cave. We'll just have to hope they've left a trail."

As Glitch silently cursed his own stupidity, Anderson opened one of the black cases. Inside were four small backpacks. She pulled out a couple and checked them over. "These are one-person packs. They're small, but they contain enough food and water for a week or so, plus flares, climbing wires, gloves, that sort of thing. They're waterproof as well, just in case."

"Any weapons?"

"No. The U.S. Air Force is not in the habit of leaving weapons lying around unguarded. Not intentionally, anyway."

Anderson picked up the packs and handed one to Glitch. It was heavier than it looked. She rummaged around inside the boxes and retrieved a heavy, rubberized flashlight.

"It's waterproof," she said, handing it to Glitch.

He went to put it in his pack then thought better of it and clipped it to his belt. As they put on their backpacks, Glitch looked at the remains of the gateway. "Hang on. This Smith guy was only a few seconds ahead of you. How did he rig that thing to explode so quickly?"

"He didn't."

"So... you guys did?"

Anderson nodded. "In case there was someone on this side of the gateway we didn't want getting through to Earth."

"Like aliens?"

"Like aliens. You ready?"

"Player one is ready," Glitch said then blushed when he realized just how nerdy he'd just sounded.

Anderson smiled then turned and walked into the tunnel. Glitch rapped his knuckles on his forehead and cursed under his breath—he was such a loser. Shaking his head, he hurried after Anderson before her flashlight vanished out of sight completely.

The corridor was narrow at first, forcing them to walk in single file. Gradually, as it curved subtly to the right and sloped upward, it widened until they could travel side by side. Their flashlights cut through the darkness, illuminating the red rock ahead of them. The walls were uneven, pitted and scarred as though the corridor had been carved out by some sort of machine or creature rather than by nature. The flashlights cast complex, irregular shadows across the walls. Three times, Glitch stumbled on the uneven surface, prompting more silent curses and self-reprimands.

Glitch wondered whether he should talk, both out of politeness and to fill the silence that seemed to be growing more and more awkward as they moved slowly along the corridor. Eventually he decided not to say anything. Captain Anderson wasn't speaking, and based on his conversational efforts so far, it was probably better for him not to try.

Anderson picked up the pace, striding ahead of Glitch. His pack was growing heavier as the minutes ticked by, and he felt the impact of a life spent sitting in front of a computer. He tried to ignore the discomfort, focusing instead on the tunnel. There didn't seem to be any turns or other routes, but the tunnel was climbing. He hoped it would lead them to the surface. Then they might be able to work out where they were, although it might also make it a lot harder to find Doctor Zheng.

Glitch was again considering trying to make conversation when they reached another cave. It was bigger than the last one, with a high, curved ceiling. It was also split down the middle by a chasm.

The gap was wide, certainly too far to jump, and when they directed their flashlights into it, blackness quickly swallowed up the light. There was no telling how deep it was, and there was no way to get around it. The dust at its edge had been disturbed, maybe by human feet—it was hard to tell. Their side of the gap was wide and smooth, but the other side was more like a ledge and peppered with lumps of rock.

"We could go back," said Glitch. "Maybe we missed a side corridor."

Anderson shook her head. "We didn't. With the gateway gone, this is the only way out, and we don't want to stay in these caves any longer than we need to."

As if the cave were emphasizing the point, the floor gave a brief shudder and rumbled.

"What was that?" asked Glitch.

"An earthquake. The first party noticed them when they came through."

Glitch eyed the rock above them. "So this place might collapse?"

Anderson opened up her backpack and pulled out a length of metal wire with a smooth cylinder attached to one end. She released a catch, and three curved metal arms popped out with a loud click.

"Is that what I think it is?" said Glitch.

"If you think it's a grappling hook, yes."

"It looks a bit… fragile."

"Looks can be deceptive. It's a titanium-molybdenum alloy. It's light but very strong. More than enough to carry our weight."

Anderson unrolled the loop, coiling it on the floor so that it would flow freely. She told Glitch to hold the end without the grappling hook. Terrified he'd drop it and lose the wire, he gripped it with both hands until his knuckles turned white.

Getting the hook across the chasm was relatively easy, but it took Anderson three attempts to wedge it behind a cluster of rocks on the other side. She pulled on the wire, leaning back with all her weight. The hook shifted slightly but held firm. She pulled a titanium stake from her backpack and secured the other end of the line to their side of the gap.

Glitch stared at the remarkably flimsy-looking wire. It didn't look safe.

"You'll need some gloves," said Captain Anderson. "To save your hands. There's a pair in your backpack. Have you ever crawled along a rope before?"

Glitch swung his pack off his back and rummaged around for the gloves. "No."

"It's not hard, but you need to hook your legs together over the wire and move as quickly as you can so your arms don't get too tired."

Glitch looked at the wire, trying not to look as terrified as he felt.

"Come on," said Anderson. "You first."

Glitch made a great show of examining the zipper and pockets on his backpack, checking and rechecking to make sure everything was secure. Then he pulled on his leather gloves, walked to the ledge, and knelt. He was thankful he had what his sister called a "maddeningly fast metabolism" and didn't weigh much. But still, the wire looked very thin and the chasm very wide. What worried him even more, though, was how he'd get on, and off, the wire.

Anderson knelt beside him. "It'll be better if you don't drag it out," she said quietly.

Glitch nodded and took a deep breath. Feet first seemed like the easiest way to travel. It took him a couple of attempts to settle on a strategy for getting onto the wire. In the end, he sat on the edge of the rock, wrapped his legs around the wire, and scooted along.

His legs slipped over the edge, and he slid awkwardly out into open air. The wire sagged, and his stomach flipped over as he felt the depths below pulling at him. He closed his eyes and gritted his teeth. He waited until both he and the wire had stopped swinging and he'd regained control of his stomach before opening his eyes and starting across.

He was smart enough not to look down. The opening

scenes of Stallone's *Cliffhanger* had taught him what happened to people who did that. The wire wobbled and shook as he slid along, but he made good progress.

Getting off the wire wasn't as easy.

By the time he'd reached the far side of the gap, his arms and legs were burning, and he was grateful for the leather gloves. Even with them, he could feel the thin wire digging into his soft programmer's hands.

The best strategy for getting back to the safety of solid ground, he decided, was to transfer from the wire to the craggy cliff face. He'd spent a couple of hours on a climbing wall as part of a tedious team-building exercise a few years back, and he saw plenty of hand and footholds he could use. But that meant hanging from the wire while he found a safe place to put his feet. He wasn't sure how long he could manage that.

Glitch got as close to the end of the wire as he could, then he unhooked his legs. For a few terrifying seconds, he thought he was too far away, but the tips of his toes touched rock. He found just enough purchase to take some of his weight and allow him to slide farther along the wire. Once he'd found more secure footholds and was as sure as he could be that he wouldn't fall, he reached out with one hand and grabbed a likely looking chunk of rock. He pulled on it a couple of times to make sure it was solid, then he chose a second handhold and let go of the wire.

He clung to the rock face for a few seconds, trying to convince himself he wasn't really on some sort of alien planet. He was just hanging a few feet above a soft foam mat in the Raleigh Mall with his safety harness firmly attached to the ceiling. When his right foot slipped, sending lumps of rock cascading into the chasm, he gave up trying to fool himself and clambered up the rock face. By the time he was lying on solid ground, staring at the ceiling, his hands were slick with sweat and his heart was hammering. He half expected it to do a John Hurt and burst out of his chest.

"Well done," called Captain Anderson. "I'm coming over."

Presumably thanks to her Air Force training, Captain Anderson swung confidently onto the wire and moved smoothly along it. Glitch watched her make her way across like a particularly sprightly caterpillar crawling along the underside of a branch. She made good progress, but as she reached the halfway mark, there was another quiet rumble and the ground shook. The movement lasted longer than before, and Glitch found himself clutching at the ground. Dust drifted down from the ceiling.

The wire vibrated, threatening to shake Anderson free. The grappling hook shifted as part of the rock it was jammed against gave way.

"Captain… errm… Scarlett, I think you'd better get moving," Glitch said. "I don't know how much longer that grappling hook will hold out."

Anderson answered by picking up her pace. A few seconds later, another even bigger quake hit. Dust and rock fragments fell from the ceiling, and a sliver of the wall broke away and crashed into the chasm, taking a chunk of the ledge with it.

Glitch looked at the grappling hook. The outcrop was breaking apart. All that was left was a solitary chunk of rock sticking up from the ground like a splintered tooth, and the grappling hook had caught against it. It looked secure as long as the rock didn't break. Slowly, the quake died away.

The grappling hook held, and Glitch let out a sigh of relief. "The line's still okay, but hurry."

As Anderson dragged herself forward again, there was a loud crack, the sound of shattering rock. The metal stake on the opposite side of the cave tore itself out of the ground.

The wire gave way, and Anderson fell.

CHAPTER THREE
Chasm of Catastrophe

Glitch finds himself trapped inside an unstable cave system with Air Force Captain Scarlett Anderson. With their only way home destroyed, they begin searching for Doctor Zheng, the head of the project that discovered the gateway and hostage of a man known only as John Smith. As Glitch and the captain search for her, they find their route blocked by a deep chasm. Using a metal line, Glitch successfully gets across, but as Anderson follows him, an earthquake hits.

Glitch looked at the grappling hook. The rock it was wedged against had broken apart. All that was left was a solitary chunk sticking up from the ground like a splintered tooth. The grappling hook looked secure as long as the rock didn't break. Slowly, the quake died away.

The grappling hook held, and Glitch let out a sigh of relief. "The line's still okay, but hurry."

As Anderson dragged herself along the wire, there was a loud crack, the sound of shattering rock, and the metal stake on the opposite side of the chasm ripped itself out of the ground.

The wire gave way, and Anderson fell.

Glitch watched in horror as Captain Anderson slammed into the cliff face with a grunt. The impact jarred her hands free. She slipped. Anderson clutched at the metal lifeline, but she was falling too fast. The wire hummed through her leather gloves, and the friction slowed her descent a little but not enough to stop her. One of her feet caught on a rocky outcrop. The impact twisted her sideways, her hands came away from the wire, and she was free-falling.

"Captain!" screamed Glitch.

Anderson's eyes met his. Where Glitch had expected fear, he saw only determination.

When Anderson reached the end of the wire, she grabbed at the remains of the metal stake. Glitch held his breath as her fingers wrapped around it. The wire snapped tight. Glitch had visions of Anderson's arms popping free of their sockets. She yelled in pain, but her arms remained attached to her body.

Anderson ducked her head out of the way as she hit the wall again. This time she held on. The wire swung, spinning her around until she managed to get a foothold on the wall.

Glitch let out his breath. "Are you okay?"

"It's all good," shouted Anderson.

"Hold on!" Glitch muttered to himself as he ran to the grappling hook, "What else is she going to do?" The hook looked secure enough—as long as there weren't any more earthquakes. He called down to Anderson, "I can try to pull you up."

There was a low-pitched rumble from somewhere deep below them, and the ground shuddered.

"Okay," said Anderson, although her tone made it clear she didn't hold out much hope.

She was right. Glitch managed to pull the wire upward a few inches, but his hands kept slipping. He was more likely to slide it sideways and dislodge the grappling hook than pull the captain to safety. After a handful of attempts, he called to her, "I think it would be better if you climbed up. If you can."

"That's what I was thinking."

Anderson examined the cliff wall for a moment then grabbed the nearest rock with one hand. She pulled at it, testing its strength. In one fluid movement, she let go of the wire and grabbed another handhold.

Glitch watched helplessly as Anderson made the ascent. The rock was rough, with plenty of places for her to hold on, but still the climb was slow. Anderson stopped to test every handhold before she put her weight on it, and with good reason. Several times the rock crumbled and broke away as soon as she pulled at it.

Anderson was twenty feet from the top of the cliff when the next quake hit. The ground vibrated beneath Glitch, and he found himself clutching at the ground again. A few chunks of rock broke free from the roof and bounced into the darkness. One of them careened off the cliff near Anderson's head, and she yelled.

As the quake died away, Anderson pulled herself up to the next handhold, but as she lifted her foot to move to a narrow ledge sticking out of the cliff, the handhold broke apart. She slipped, her feet flailing in mid-air until they found purchase again. She clutched at the rock, grabbing another handhold. It crumbled slightly but held.

Glitch was more than a little relieved when Anderson finally reached the top of the ledge. He helped her onto solid ground, then he stood back, wondering what to do next.

Anderson lay on her back, her breathing heavy. Eventually, she managed a smile. "That was fun." The ground shuddered again. "We should get away from the ledge."

Glitch moved toward her, but she was up before he could work out how to help. She recovered the wire, unhooked the grapple, coiled it up, and replaced it in her backpack. There was only one way off the ledge—another tunnel. As they walked toward it, the ground gave a slight shudder, one last aftershock to send them on their way.

The new passage tunnel was bigger than its twin—at least twice as wide and almost as high. The walls were scarred and chipped, but the damage had been done in bigger, broader strokes. Glitch ran his fingers over the wall. Maybe whatever had drilled or clawed out the tunnel on this side of the chasm was bigger.

They walked in silence for about ten minutes before they reached a junction. The tunnel they were in turned right, but two smaller passages wound off to the left like tributaries feeding a river. They stuck to the larger of the three routes, but a few hundred feet later, it split again. This time, there was no obvious main path.

Glitch flicked his flashlight down the tunnels, right then left. The first seemed empty, but as the light drove away the shadows in the second, he thought he saw something move across the rock wall. He didn't mention it to Anderson—he was almost sure he'd imagined it, and he didn't want to sound like a frightened child. Still, he wasn't happy when Anderson scratched an arrow into the wall and led them down the left-hand tunnel.

"Why left?" he asked.

"My dad always told me that if I wasn't sure which direction to take, left would never let me down."

Glitch pondered that for a moment, not really sure what it meant. In the end, he settled for a slight shrug and followed Anderson. As Glitch hurried to catch up, his flashlight caught the edge of something moving across the wall. "Did you see that?"

Anderson opened her mouth to reply then froze, grabbing Glitch's shoulder. "Don't move."

She swept her flashlight across the wall. It was moving. Hundreds, maybe even thousands of bulbous red slugs scurried across the wall, chased away by the light. Their skin was so close to the color of the surrounding rock that the wall itself seemed alive. Glitch had seen slugs like that in the forests near his home, but whereas those had dragged themselves slowly across rocks and gravel paths, these creatures moved quickly, more like cockroaches than slugs.

Something dropped from the ceiling, flashing past a few inches from Glitch's face. He raised his flashlight. The ceiling was covered with slugs writhing and sliding over each other. As he watched, another of the creatures dropped from the ceiling. Then a third. That one landed on his hand. He felt a burning sensation, and he yelped, jerking his hand violently to the right and sending the creature arcing into the wall. There was a broad red welt across the back of his hand, and it already itched.

"Come on," said Anderson, pulling Glitch backward.

He didn't need more encouragement. They backed away as more and more of the creatures fell. The slug-things scattered when they hit the floor, slithering off in all directions, but far too many were advancing toward Glitch and Anderson. They turned and ran, rushing back along the tunnel until the slugs were out of sight.

Glitch looked warily at his hand. The red line seemed to have darkened, and he felt as if thousands of ants, all of which had tiny light sabers attached to their feet, were crawling over his hand. He waved his other hand over the mark, hoping the mere proximity of it would ease some of his discomfort. It didn't, and he had to pull his hand back before he succumbed to the intense desire to claw at it.

"Don't think about it," said Anderson, sounding suspiciously like his mother. "It will only itch more."

She swung her pack off her back, unzipped the front pocket, and took out a small red bag marked with a white cross. She flipped it open, retrieved a small metal cylinder slightly larger than a lipstick, and handed it to him. "Spray it with this—it might help."

It took Glitch a couple of attempts to find the tiny opening on the canister because he was holding it upside down. He turned it the right way up, aimed it at his hand, and pressed the top. A fine mist coated the back of his hand, and he sighed with relief as the cool spray washed away the itching sensation.

Glitch offered Anderson the spray. "Thank you."

"Keep it. There's another one in your pack if you need more."

Glitch slipped the tube into his pocket. He imagined he could already feel the ants returning. At least, he hoped he was only imagining it.

They retraced their steps, and when they got back to the junction, Anderson scratched out the mark she'd made on the wall. She drew another arrow, this time pointing right. "Apparently my dad didn't know as much as he thought he did."

"Was he in the Air Force too?"

"No, he was a fireman."

"Oh, cool. I always wanted to be a fireman. I liked hoses when I was a kid."

Anderson pressed her lips together in an attempt to stop herself from laughing. She failed and burst into a deep, husky laugh that echoed off the walls. Glitch liked the sound of it. It was a warm laugh, uninhibited despite their predicament.

Then he realized why she was laughing, and he blushed. "I mean… I liked playing—" He shut his mouth before he could dig himself any deeper.

Eventually, Anderson wiped away a tear and shook her head slowly. "I'm sorry, Dw—Glitch."

He smiled, hoping to give Anderson the impression he was self-confident enough to be able to laugh at himself. "Don't worry about it."

At least her laughter proved she had a sense of humor. And she'd liked his T-shirt. Unless that had been sarcasm, of course.

"Come on," said Anderson, shaking her head.

They continued on. A few minutes later, the tunnel opened up into a large cave. Anderson raised her hand, fist clenched, and stopped. Glitch was busy watching the ceiling for more slugs, and he almost ran into her before he realized what she meant.

The cave was much bigger than the one they'd arrived in. Hundreds of spheres lined the walls. Some were slightly bigger than a beach ball, while others were the size of Glitch's fist. They glowed, casting a soft, phosphorescent blue light across the room. The floor was dark brown, almost black, and it was dirt rather than red rock. Scattered around the room were a dozen mounds of dirt, like molehills, but each was a foot high and at least three feet across. The air was thick with an ammonia smell, and there were dark patches in the dirt around the edges of the room. There was no sign of whatever had made the mounds.

41

"They must have really big moles here," said Glitch.

Anderson glared and slashed her hand across her throat. Glitch flinched. She was concentrating on one of the mounds near the center of the room. To Glitch, it looked like all the others, medium-sized and unremarkable.

Then he saw it.

The sides of the mound were moving, sending tiny avalanches of dirt cascading down its slopes. Instinctively, Glitch stepped backward. A lump of earth broke away from the top of the mound and rolled down its side. Glitch frowned. He thought he heard a noise but not from the cave—from somewhere behind them. It had sounded like someone dragging a pitchfork over the rock. He placed his hand lightly on Anderson's shoulder. She started to shrug him off, then the noise came again. Louder. Nearer. As one, they turned, the shifting mound forgotten.

The creature advancing toward them down the tunnel looked like a four-legged metallic crab, roughly three feet high. Its ovoid body was mottled red, green, and blue, and it shimmered in the light of their flashlights. A handful of lumps and rough patches were scattered across its surface, like scabs.

Its legs were thick and heavy near the body, tapering to a narrow point where they touched the ground. But it was the creature's arms that made Glitch most nervous. It had two arms, like a normal crab, but rather than pincers, these looked like the serrated knives you'd find in an upmarket steakhouse, but they were almost two feet long.

Three blue orbs, similar to the ones lining the walls of the room, grew from the thing's back. They cast eerie shadows that stretched and distorted on the tunnel walls as the creature moved. Glitch couldn't see any eyes, but any of those lumps could be some sort of armored eyeball.

The crab waved its arms as it marched steadily toward them. Anderson and Glitch backed into the cave, away from the creature. Glitch risked a quick glance over his shoulder. There was an exit on the opposite side. If the creature wasn't too fast, they could make it.

They were near the center of the room when the creature stopped moving, slammed the points of its steak-knife arms into the floor like a gorilla pounding the ground, and screeched. Its body reverberated with the effort as the glass-shatteringly high-pitched cry drilled straight into Glitch's skull. He flinched and pressed his hands against his ears. Anderson did the same.

A few seconds later, another screech, this one quieter, muffled, came from somewhere behind them. They turned. Glitch swore as a long metallic blade rose from a nearby mound. A mound that lay directly between them and the exit.

CHAPTER FOUR
Claws of Fear

After narrowly avoiding death crossing the underground chasm, Glitch and Captain Anderson continue their search for Doctor Zheng. Their path is blocked by an infestation of acido slugs and they are forced to back track, only to find themselves under attack from a giant crab-like creature.

The creature slammed the points of its steak-knife arms into the ground and screeched. Its body reverberated with the effort as its high-pitched cry drilled into Glitch's skull. He clamped his hands over his ears, trying to stop the sound from tearing him apart. Anderson did the same.

Another screech came from somewhere behind them, this one muffled. They turned. Glitch cursed as a long metallic blade eased out from behind a nearby mound of earth. A mound that lay directly between them and the exit.

Another crab hauled itself from the hole. It was about half the size of the first but looked no less dangerous. It shook, dislodging a few pockets of dirt that had become trapped between the wart-like growths on its body. Knife-blade arms sliced through the air as it stalked toward them, emitting another piercing cry. The larger creature—Glitch imagined it was the mother or father—called in return and slammed the points of its arms into the ground, cracking the rock.

Glitch looked desperately toward the exit, but it was too far. If those creatures decided to attack, there wasn't much they could do. "Any ideas?"

"Just one." Without taking her eyes off the creatures, Anderson opened Glitch's backpack and dug around inside.

The smaller creature took a couple of quick steps toward them.

"You might want to hurry up," said Glitch.

Anderson ignored him as she withdrew three tubes. They were red with bright yellow caps on one end.

"Is that dynamite?" said Glitch.

Anderson rolled her eyes. "We're not in a Clint Eastwood movie."

She pulled the cap from one of the tubes, and the flare burst to life. Anderson threw it toward the smaller of the two creatures. The flare bounced across the floor, trailing smoke. The crab cried out and skittered sideways, away from the sputtering flame. Behind them, the larger creature let out a long screech. Anderson turned, lit another flare, and tossed it at its feet. The bigger creature reared up, and its claws clipped the ceiling, dislodging a few chunks of rock. It scuttled backward.

Anderson lit the last flare and threw it halfway between the smaller creature and the exit. It caught on one of the mounds and fell short. She grabbed Glitch's arm. "Come on."

She pulled him sideways, moving farther away from both the creatures and the exit. Smoke from the flares filled the air, making Glitch cough. The smaller creature was growing more and more agitated, stamping its feet and emitting shrill, plaintive cries.

Glitch looked back at the crab in the tunnel. It had approached the flare again. It stretched out one of its claws and flicked at the tube, sending it rolling across the ground. With the threat gone, it moved back into the cave, let out three short, sharp cries, then charged toward them.

"Run!" shouted Anderson, yanking Glitch toward the exit.

They sprinted across the soft earth, dodging the mounds and hoping more of the creatures weren't waiting to snatch them underground as they passed. Anderson let go of Glitch's arm and veered to the left. Confused by the sudden change of plan, Glitch missed his footing and tripped. He sprawled to the ground, landing right beside one of the bigger mounds. The earth beside his face shifted, and he saw a flash of metal inside the hole. Terror swept over him, more intense than anything he'd ever felt. He pushed himself to his feet.

Anderson had retrieved one of the flares and was

standing at the exit. "Come on!"

Not daring to look back, Glitch ran toward Anderson and the relative safety of the tunnels. As he passed her, she stepped forward and dropped the flare in the mouth of the tunnel.

"Keep going," she said.

Together, they ran along the passageway, the harsh cries of the crabs echoing around them.

They continued running until Glitch thought he might throw up. He slowed then stopped and bent over, resting his hands on his knees. "Hold on… I need… a rest."

Anderson checked the tunnel behind them then nodded. She pulled out a canteen of water and handed it to Glitch. "I don't think they're coming after us."

Glitch gulped at the water. "What were they?"

"Your guess is as good as mine. Alien planet, remember?"

There was a quiet rumble from somewhere beneath their feet, and the ground shuddered. Thin trickles of dust drifted down on them.

"You're sure this is another planet, then?"

"As far as we can tell, yes. The air here is similar to Earth. It's breathable, obviously, but there's slightly less oxygen, although that could be due to altitude. Gravity is a bit higher as well."

"That explains why I got so tired running."

"Yeah… that explains it."

Glitch pushed himself upright and handed the canteen back to Anderson. He hesitated, not sure whether he wanted to know the answer to his next question. "So if no one from Earth has been here before, who built the gateway?"

"That," said Anderson, her eyebrows raised, "is the billion-dollar question."

Glitch wondered if they would be the ones to answer it. First contact with an intelligent alien race was something he'd only ever seen in movies. He wasn't sure he was the right person for the job—he was no Jodie Foster and not just for the obvious reasons.

He started to ask Anderson if she'd been trained for close encounters of an alien kind, but she held up her hand. "Can you hear that?"

He couldn't at first. Then he caught the sound. Running water. "An underground river?"

"It would make sense. Those crab things probably need to drink." Anderson hooked the canteen onto her belt. "You okay to carry on now?"

Ignoring the jelly-like consistency of his legs, Glitch nodded.

The sound of water grew louder as they moved through the tunnels, and before long, they found themselves in another cavern. Thousands of gallons of water poured from an opening in the rock wall far above them to crash into an oval lake that took up most of the cavern. The walls were covered with those blue phosphorescent globes. There were dozens of them on the wall behind the waterfall, making it glow. A fine mist hung in the air, cool and moist. They stood for a moment, watching the foaming, writhing water at the fall's base.

Anderson said something, but the roar of the water made it impossible for him to hear what she'd said. He cupped a hand over his ear and shook his head. They walked along the lake shore until they were far enough away that they could talk comfortably.

Anderson looked back along the lake at the glowing blue falls. "It's beautiful."

Glitch nodded, resisting the urge to make some sort of comparison between her and the waterfall. No doubt it would just come out wrong and he'd end up insulting her. He also resisted making a joke about needing to pee.

The water in the lake was perfectly clear, and Glitch could see the lake bed. It dropped steeply away from the shore, the water quickly becoming too deep to see the bottom, the red rock replaced by inky blackness. From what Glitch could tell, there was no plant or animal life in the water, but who knew what was lurking beneath the surface? Thinking of the giant crabs, Glitch stepped backward, away from the edge of the lake.

"Any signs of life?" said Anderson.

"Not that I can see, but it looks pretty deep."

Anderson pointed at the other side of the cave. "There're at least three ways out of here. If they came this way, they could have taken any of them."

"Was Zheng's dad a fireman?" asked Glitch.

Anderson frowned.

"Maybe they went with the left tunnel," said Glitch.

"Ah… I see. We're back onto hoses again."

Glitch felt himself blush then blush harder as his stomach growled. He shifted his feet, hoping the movement would discourage any further intestinal outbursts.

"Maybe we should have something to eat before we carry on," said Anderson.

Glitch nodded, and they took off their packs and sat. That something was a protein bar—peanut butter crisp with a chocolate-flavored coating, according to the foil wrapper. The food was as solid as a brick and had a faint chemical under-taste, but it wasn't terrible. They ate and drank in silence, both of them enjoying the unexpected beauty of the underground lake. Glitch could almost imagine he was in some secluded area of a national park on Earth, not trapped on an alien planet with no way to get home and any number of hostile creatures out to eat him.

As Glitch washed down the final piece of protein bar, he stopped. The wall opposite them had changed, he was sure of it. When they'd sat down, it had been flat. Now it had a round bulge at about head height. As he watched, the bulge grew larger.

"Ah, crap," he whispered.

Anderson was staring at the wall too, her eyes narrowed. The bulge moved again, sliding slowly to its left. Then it popped backward, disappearing out of sight. A few seconds later, the bulge reappeared higher up the rock face and to the right. It stayed there for a moment then vanished again.

"It looks like something out of *The Haunting of Hill House*," said Glitch.

"I don't think it's a ghost."

The bulge reappeared right in front of them and steadily grew larger. It was almost perfectly spherical; only the natural cracks and fissures in the rock lent it any texture at all. Two horizontal slits appeared in the sphere, about a third of the way down its surface. The slits opened, revealing two black circles—eyeballs. The bulge blinked twice then retreated into the rock.

"Something's living in the wall," said Glitch.

He was grateful when Anderson didn't point out how obvious his comment was, but as if to prove his point, the face reappeared, its eyes already open. A horizontal slit appeared, turning rapidly into a mouth with the corners turned upward in what looked suspiciously like a smile. Thick eyebrows waggled above the black eyes.

"Hello," said Glitch.

The rock-thing tipped its head sideways, blinked, then vanished back into the wall. Moments later, it surfaced in the floor a couple of feet in front of Glitch. He smiled and crouched down to get a closer look, but as he moved, the creature jerked backward, staying just out of reach. Its smile grew wider. It sank back into the rock and popped into view again after a few seconds, this time to their right.

"It's playing with us," said Anderson.

"I wonder if he has a name?"

"He?"

"It looks like a he to me."

The creature tilted its head and let out a short, sharp grunt. Almost a bark.

"Well, he sounds like a dog," said Anderson.

"Fido it is, then."

"Fido?"

"Sure, why not?"

Anderson rolled her eyes and gave a little shake of her head. Glitch laughed and jumped forward as though he was going to try to grab the creature. It let out a startled growl and pulled back, lifting itself out of the ground. Two thick arms appeared, quickly followed by two huge fists. Fido pushed himself upward, forcing his body out of the rock and sending red dust billowing into the air. He dragged himself upright on two legs as thick as tree trunks and stepped forward. Glitch stumbled backward as he tried to avoid getting stepped on. His feet caught on something, and he fell backward into the lake.

The water was cold. Shock forced the air from his lungs, and his mouth filled with water. He kicked, thrashing his arms and legs, panic overwhelming his instincts for a few seconds. He sank like a stone until his back hit rock. He reached around to push himself upward then realized the rock was raising him back toward the surface. He felt it shifting around him, forming and reforming to fit his body.

His feet found the shallow edge of the lake as he broke the surface. Looking back into the water, he saw Fido looking up at him as he lifted Glitch to safety. When Glitch was standing on his own two feet, the creature retreated into the depths of the lake and disappeared. Anderson stood near the edge of the lake, trying not to laugh. Glitch looked at her and raised his eyebrows.

"I'm sorry," she said. "You look like a bedraggled little dog."

"I'm more of a cat person, and cats really don't like water."

Glitch held out his hand toward Anderson. As her fingertips touched his, something slick and cold wrapped around his ankle. He lunged toward Anderson, clutching at her hand. He'd almost gotten a hold of it when he was yanked back into the water.

CHAPTER FIVE
Lake Terror

Fleeing an encounter with a pair of metallic crab-like creatures, Glitch and Captain Anderson discover an underground waterfall and lake. While resting there, they're visited by a rock creature that they christen Fido. As Glitch plays with the creature, he falls into the lake, but he is rescued by Fido.

Anderson stood near the edge of the lake, trying not to laugh. Glitch raised his eyebrows.

"I'm sorry," she said. "You look like a bedraggled little dog."

"I'm more of a cat person, and cats really don't like water."

Glitch reached out to Anderson, but as her fingers touched his, something cold and slick wrapped around his ankle. He dived forward, grabbing at Anderson's hand. He'd almost gotten a hold of it when he was yanked back into the water.

Water swamped Glitch's face again. It filled his nose and mouth as he was dragged under. Fighting down the panic that threatened to drown him, he pried at the thick, rubbery tentacle wrapped around his leg. His fingers slipped across the slick skin. He kicked, trying to swim upward.

His head broke the surface of the lake again, and he dragged a mouthful of air into his lungs. He thought he heard Anderson calling to him, but her voice was drowned out as the creature pulled him back beneath the water. It dragged him along the lake, toward the waterfall.

Again he tried to pry himself free, and this time his fingers found a way between his leg and the tentacle. But as he dug his fingers into the soft flesh, the creature tightened its grip. Glitch had visions of his foot popping off the end of his leg and pulled his hand back. His lungs were starting to burn. He tried to stretch upward, to poke his head into the air that was maddeningly close, but the buffeting of the water made it impossible.

The creature turned again, aiming for the middle of the lake. Stars burst across Glitch's eyes as blackness seeped in at the edges of his vision. Glitch saw the waterfall a few feet ahead, and he wondered if the creature was going to bludgeon him against the wall behind it. Maybe that was its way of killing its food before eating it. He braced himself for the impact, hoping the lack of oxygen would make him black out before he slammed into the rock.

His head surfaced just as he hit the waterfall. Razor-sharp ribbons of water stung his face. He dragged in another breath, catching a mouthful of ice-cold water at the same time. Then he was past the cascading water and dragged through an uneven slot in the rock that stopped just above the waterline. He'd been lucky not to smash his skull on the way through.

The creature slowed. The tentacle around Glitch's leg loosened then let go completely, leaving him treading water in total darkness.

It sounded as though he was in another cavern. He heard the water lapping against the walls around him, but there were none of the blue phosphorescent spheres to provide light. He could almost feel the walls closing in on him in the pitch black.

Glitch took a deep breath, trying to quell the claustrophobia growing inside him. He'd never been good with enclosed spaces. He closed his eyes then opened them again. That only made things worse. There was a splash to his right, and a moment later, something brushed against his thigh. He jerked away, his heart racing.

He had no idea how to get out of the cave. He could hear the waterfall, but the sound echoed off the walls, obscuring which direction it was coming from. He looked around, desperately trying to find the gap in the rock he'd been dragged through. Surely there was enough light in the other cave to give him some sort of idea of which direction to swim in?

Glitch groaned.

"Idiot," he snapped, the sound bouncing around the cavern.

He reached down, searching for his flashlight and trying to remember whether it was attached to his belt or stuffed in his backpack. He'd almost given up when his fingers wrapped around the rubber body of the light. Clutching it tightly in one hand, he unclipped it with the other. Glitch took a breath as he lifted the flashlight above the surface and flicked the switch.

Nothing happened.

How could the Air Force's waterproof flashlights not be waterproof? He cycled the switch on and off a couple of times, and the flashlight flickered to life.

He'd been right. He was in a cavern much smaller than the one containing the lake, but it was still high enough that his meager flashlight struggled to illuminate the ceiling. Where it did, the light glinted off the rock, reflected by thousands of tiny crystals that floated overhead like stars in the night sky. Like the rest of the tunnel system, the walls were chipped and scraped, and the overall shape of the room was too uniform for Glitch to believe it was anything other than man made. Or alien made.

There was another splash, and Glitch remembered where he was—treading water in a lake of indeterminate depth, filled with an indeterminate number of potentially lethal alien species. He swung his light around the edge of the lake and found a sloped beach leading out of the water. He kicked out toward it, his splashing echoing off the ceiling and fortunately drowning out the sound of any approaching life forms. He kept the flashlight in his hand, but after a few strokes, he turned it off. The erratic movement of the light cast disturbing shadows across the walls that made him even less comfortable with his predicament.

Something bumped his leg. He kicked harder. His arms and legs were tiring from the effort of the swim, but the beach was only a few feet away. It was indeed made of sand. Red sand but sand nonetheless. Ignoring the burning in his muscles, he kicked again. His hands touched something. Something slick. It slithered away from his fingers.

Glitch stopped swimming. He didn't want to end up in the path of another of those creatures, but he was equally reluctant to stay in the water. As his feet drifted downward, they touched the bottom of the lake. Standing on tiptoe, he flicked on the flashlight and swept it across the water. The lake seemed empty. He walked toward the shore as quickly as he could, swinging the flashlight in front of him. The water grew shallow, and soon he was wading across the beach, water spraying from his arms and legs as he hurried toward the safety of dry land.

The beach ended in a ramp carved from the ever-present red rock. If there had been any doubts in Glitch's mind that something other than nature had created this cavern, that ramp dispelled them. It curved smoothly away from the beach and wound up the wall, disappearing into the darkness. The ramp was basically smooth, but two thin tracks ran along the middle of it, the edges worn and chipped.

Something splashed in the pool, far enough away that Glitch felt safe to shine his flashlight across the water. Maybe he'd finally see what had dragged him here.

Instead, he saw Anderson gliding through the water toward him, her flashlight bobbing in the darkness. Glitch shouted to her, urging her on as he frantically scanned the cave for signs of the creatures. The thick black body of something sinister broke the surface a few feet away from Anderson. It curved through the water, turning toward her.

"Come on!" screamed Glitch, waving his flashlight above his head like an air traffic controller.

The panic in his voice must have gotten through to Anderson, because her flashlight dipped below the water as she ducked her head forward and pushed toward shore. Her light glowed beneath the lake, creating an eerie circle around Anderson as she swam. Glitch saw dark shadows flitting through the water near her, darting away from the light then drifting cautiously back toward Anderson again.

She was less than fifteen feet from shore when the black shape reappeared, looming up out of the water behind her. Glitch swung his flashlight upward, following the thick black body of the creature until the light reached its head. To the ten-year-old hiding inside Glitch, it looked like a really ugly dinosaur.

Two bulbous eyes, black and cold like a shark's, stuck out of the sides of an elongated, pitted head. Its mouth was so wide, it seemed to split the creature's head almost in two. Dozens of long, twisted teeth poked out of the sides of the split at weird angles.

Glitch aimed his flashlight at the creature's head, trying desperately to buy Anderson some more time. It let out a hoarse cry, almost a growl, and reared backward away from the light. Glitch chased it with the beam, aiming it at the thing's eyes in the hope that living so long in the darkness of the lake had left it unable to handle bright light. The creature thrashed and writhed as it fought to escape the light. Another black shape rose out of the water—its tail. The tail slapped back down on the surface of the pool, barely missing Anderson's legs. The monster growled again.

Glitch glanced at the beach. Anderson was standing now, wading through water that barely reached her waist. A few seconds more and she'd be safe. He waved the flashlight frantically at the creature's head, but this time, it ignored the light. Its mouth opened, revealing three more rows of disfigured teeth. A long black tongue probed the air, viscous gray goo dripping from its tip. It lunged toward the captain.

"Look out!" shouted Glitch.

Without looking back, Anderson dodged left, throwing herself sideways as the creature's head slammed into the water where she'd just been standing. It whipped its head backward for another strike, but Anderson didn't give it a second chance. She dragged herself through the water, staggering forward as she got to her feet and ran up the slope. A few seconds later, she was standing next to Glitch. The lake monster let out a frustrated bellow.

"Are you okay?" asked Anderson.

Glitch looked at her, eyebrows raised. "Me? Are *you* okay?"

Anderson grinned. "Couldn't be better."

Glitch studied her for a moment. She looked pale but barely out of breath, as though she'd been swimming lengths in her local pool rather than escaping from an alien water serpent with murderous intentions. She didn't have her pack with her.

"I don't suppose there's any more of those Air Force backpacks lying around?"

Instinctively, Anderson reached toward her shoulder where her pack would have been. She grimaced. "No, sorry."

He shook his head and pointed his flashlight toward the ramp. "That's the only way out. Unless you want to go for another swim and get those packs."

Anderson turned back toward the lake, feigning indecision. "No, I think we'll stick to dry land for the time being."

"In that case, after you."

The ramp was wide enough for two of them, but the sheer drop into the pool meant Glitch was more comfortable following a few feet behind. A track had been cut into the wall just above waist height. Glitch slipped his hand into it, using it as a handrail for an extra layer of safety.

The ramp wound gradually around the pool a couple of times, taking them up so high, Glitch's stomach became very uneasy if he happened to look over the edge. The crystals Glitch had seen in the ceiling peppered the wall as well. They looked like diamonds. Big diamonds. He wondered if Anderson would let him stop and pry out a few, but she seemed focused on the path, not the potentially unlimited wealth that lay just a few inches to her left.

They followed the ramp until they were almost at the ceiling, and Glitch could stretch up and touch the tips of some of the bigger crystals. If he had a knife, he could scrape away at the rock and free enough diamonds to keep him in soda for his lifetime.

Glitch was eyeing up a long crystal roughly as thick as his thumb when Anderson tapped his shoulder. "Look."

The ramp leveled off and continued twenty or thirty feet ahead of them, cutting through the wall to form a tunnel. At the end of the tunnel sat a gateway exactly like the one they'd used to get there. The same coffin-shaped metal surrounded the same shimmering, glistening mirror-like surface. Could that be a way home?

Without a word, they hurried toward the gateway.

Glitch picked up a rock from the floor. The gateway was set into the wall, just as the others had been, and its mirrored surface shifted and twisted as they approached. It looked eager for them to step into its liquid embrace. Glitch pulled his arm back, ready to throw the rock into the gateway.

"Wait," said Anderson. "What if there's someone on the other side? Do we really want to introduce ourselves to an alien race by throwing rocks at them?"

Glitch froze. She had a point. He let the rock drop to the floor.

"I'll go first," said Anderson.

Before Glitch could answer, she moved forward, took a deep breath, and stepped into the gateway. Glitch took what he hoped was his last look at the alien world around him, clipped his flashlight to his belt, then followed her.

The journey through the gateway was shorter and less intense this time. Glitch felt himself being dragged forward as light exploded around him. An icy chill seeped into his bones, then he was through.

A wave of dizziness hit Glitch as he stepped out of the other side of the gateway and into a brightly lit room. The harsh glare was so strong he had to shield his eyes. He stood there, wavering slightly, as his stomach caught up with the rest of his body and his eyes adjusted to the light.

"Are you okay?" said Anderson.

Her voice was quiet, as though she was standing at the other end of a long corridor, but when Glitch could finally open his eyes, she was standing right next to him. He blinked a couple of times, shuddered, and nodded.

They were standing in a rectangular room—some sort of lab. It was dominated by a device that looked a lot like a giant metal hamster ball that hung above a metal disk. Two large posts stood on either side of the ball, a silver sphere on top of each one.

Every few seconds, electrical energy danced up the posts and around the spheres, occasionally leaping across to the hamster ball. A console covered with switches, dials, meters, and digital displays sat near the device. Its lights flashed green and red, and the needles on the meters flickered left and right as the electricity climbed the poles.

As it moved, the energy made a sharp crackling sound. The whole scene reminded Glitch of the set of an old black-and-white horror movie. He half expected Colin Clive to come wandering out and declare that "it" was alive.

Then he saw the figure lying within the metal cage—Doctor Zheng.

Anderson ran toward her. "Doctor!"

The doctor didn't respond. Fingers of blue-white lightning jumped from the poles to the cage again. Doctor Zheng convulsed and let out a cry. At least she was alive.

Anderson pointed at the console. "Find a way to shut it down!"

Glitch stared at the console. There were dozens of switches and dials marked with various combinations of lines and curves, none of which meant anything to him. Some of the switches were up, some were down, and there was no discernible pattern. There was no big red stop button, no giant lever that could be pulled down to disable the machine.

But one dial was bigger than the others, and it was turned all the way to the right. Assuming the controls followed the same logic as they would on Earth, it might be the power setting. Not daring to think too hard, Glitch grabbed the dial and spun it to the left.

Electricity leapt from the posts again, and the smell of burning metal filled the air.

Doctor Zheng screamed.

CHAPTER SIX
The Cage of Doom

Glitch is dragged underwater by a lake monster and taken through the waterfall into a dark cave. He manages to free himself and is relieved when Captain Anderson joins him on the lake's shore. They discover a gateway identical to the one that brought them to the planet in the first place and step through it, hoping it's a way home. Instead, they find themselves in a lab. Their companion, Doctor Zheng, is there—imprisoned inside a metal cage.

Anderson ran toward the cage. "Doctor!"

Zheng didn't move. Blue-white lightning leapt from the two poles flanking the cage and crackled across its surface. Doctor Zheng convulsed and screamed.

Anderson pointed at the console next to Glitch. "Find a way to shut it down!"

Glitch stared at the console for a moment, taking in the array of controls. He grabbed the biggest dial he saw and turned it all the way to the left. Electricity leapt from the posts again. The smell of burning metal filled the air.

Doctor Zheng screamed.

"Glitch!" shouted Anderson.

Glitch twisted the dial back to the right, but the electricity remained. His hands hovered over the controls as he tried to decide which would turn off the machine. There were dozens of switches, buttons, and silver panels, but Glitch had no idea which controlled the machine, and he was terrified of making things worse by flicking switches randomly. He looked around the room, desperately searching for a master switch, a wall socket he could unplug, or just something to smash the console with.

Apart from the gateway they'd come through and what looked like an ordinary door, the lab was empty. Thick black cables snaked across the floor between the console and the device. Glitch grabbed the cables. They were warm. He pulled at them, leaning his whole weight into the movement, but they held firm.

As Glitch pulled on them again, the door to the room slid open, and a figure entered. Glitch dropped the cable.

The figure was humanoid in shape, roughly seven feet tall. Rather than flesh and blood, it was made of a dark-blue cloud of energy, soft and amorphous. Sparks flickered within its body and danced across its arms and legs. It drifted across the room, and although its legs were moving, the motion was light, as though it was floating above the ground rather than walking on it.

The energy being approached Glitch, and the hairs on

the back of his arms stood up. Glitch backed away until his back hit the hard metal wall behind him. But the creature ignored him and moved to the console instead. It lifted its right arm and reached toward a rectangular metal plate set into the console's face. At first its hand was just an oval disk, but as it moved over the plate, it split, reconfiguring into a more human-like shape but with only three fingers.

Electricity arced between the newly created fingers and the plate. The energy rippling up the metal poles vanished almost immediately, taking the crackling noise with it. The being swept its hand across another metal plate, and the hamster ball cage lowered slowly to the ground. When it touched down, there was a hiss, and the front of the cage swung up and away.

Without hesitation, Anderson clambered inside and knelt beside Zheng. "Doctor?"

The doctor let out a low groan and tried to lift her head.

Anderson relaxed slightly but placed her hand on Zheng's shoulder. "Don't move."

She pressed her fingertips against Zheng's throat and frowned. While Anderson tended to Zheng, Glitch edged around the room toward the cage. As he moved, he watched the energy being. It stood beside the console, watching Anderson and completely ignoring Glitch.

"Is she okay?" asked Glitch when he reached the cage.

"I think so, but it's hard to tell. If that… thing hadn't arrived, she'd be dead."

"Any ideas what it is?"

Anderson gave a little laugh. Glitch cringed inside. Stupid question. The energy being moved forward. Glitch tensed. Anderson stood and put herself between Glitch and the creature.

"Is she healthy?" The being's voice was feminine and melodious, but it had a slight echo, as though they were inside a cave.

"She'll probably survive," said Anderson. "Thank you for turning off the machine."

The being gave a slight bow but didn't speak.

The silence hung in the air for several seconds before Anderson broke it. "My name is Captain Anderson. This is Doctor Zheng, and that is Glitch Mitchell."

"I am Kalith. I am Invisitude. Welcome."

Glitch stared at Kalith, not quite able to believe he was meeting an honest-to-goodness alien. Unless the conspiracy theorists were right, this was the first contact the human race had ever had with an intelligent alien race.

Anderson was more composed. "Thank you, Kalith."

Zheng coughed, and Anderson crouched down again. The doctor moved to sit up. Anderson tried to stop her, but the doctor knocked her hand away.

"Kalith—" said Zheng. Her voice was dry, cracked, and the words gave way to a round of coughing. Anderson gave her another drink from the canteen. When Zheng spoke again, her voice was clearer. "Kalith. The human race has searched for so long, hoping to find other intelligent beings. It is truly an honor to meet you."

"Thank you," said Kalith.

The floor trembled, and the metal ball creaked ominously.

"We should get out of this cage," said Anderson.

"Yes, yes," said Zheng, not taking her eyes off Kalith. "I have so many questions, I don't really know where to start."

Glitch couldn't help but smile at the excitement in Zheng's eyes.

"I understand," said Kalith. "But time limited."

"Limited? How?"

"Invisitude need help. Perhaps your help."

If Zheng had seemed excited before, now she was ecstatic. "Of course. Anything, anything at all."

"But first," said Anderson carefully, "we need to get you out of this cage."

Zheng let Anderson help her up. The two of them slowly left the machine. Zheng was a little unsteady on her feet, and she leaned heavily against Anderson as they walked.

"Are you sure you're okay?" asked Anderson.

Zheng nodded, but she looked pale.

"What happened to you? How did you end up in there?"

"The gateway led us to some caves."

"We came the same way," said Anderson.

"What about the explosives? Did he destroy the gateway?"

"Yes, we made it through just before they went off.

How did you get here?"

"He brought me through another gateway. Captain, he seemed to know exactly where he was going."

"Like he's been here before?" asked Glitch.

"That's impossible," said Anderson. "The gateway was dormant when we discovered it, and it's been guarded ever since. No one apart from the survey team has been through."

Doctor Zheng shrugged. "He knew to bring me here, and he knew how to start that machine."

Glitch ran his fingers through his hair and let out a deep breath.

Zheng looked at Glitch and frowned. "You're Dwayne Mitchell. The one who wrote about the aliens."

It was a statement rather than a question, but Glitch nodded anyway.

"Such nonsense," said Zheng. "I find it hard to believe my fellow judges voted for it."

Glitch blushed. "I… errm… prefer to be called… Glitch."

"Glitch?" said Zheng, her voice tinged with contempt. Apparently the effects of the machine were wearing off.

"Y-yes."

Zheng let out a little snort and turned away from him. She took another drink of water from the canteen and returned her attention to Kalith. The floor shook again, and a rumbling sound came from somewhere deep beneath the room.

"I apologize," said Kalith. "Time is passing."

"I'm sorry. Kalith," said Doctor Zheng, "we're wasting your time with our mundane chatter. You said you needed our assistance?"

"Yes. Invisitude require help. Kalith open gateway. Kalith guide discovery."

"You helped us find the gateway? How?"

"Provided evidence. Clues."

Questions flooded Glitch's mind. Things like "How the hell did you do that?" and "Does that mean you've been to Earth?"

"So now we're here," said Anderson. "How can we help you?"

"I will show."

Without waiting for a response, Kalith moved toward the door she'd come through. It opened as she got near, and she led Glitch, Anderson, and Zheng outside. The door opened onto a corridor made of polished metal. Harsh white lights ran along the ceiling, creating the sterile feel of a hospital but without the chemical tang of disinfectant.

Kalith turned right. Again Glitch was struck by the alien's strange, floating movements. They had a hypnotic quality to them; he couldn't stop looking. A short way down the corridor, they reached a door. It slid open as Kalith approached, and she led them inside.

Glitch had expected another corridor on the other side of the door, or another lab. Instead, they found themselves in a circular, domed room, well over two hundred feet across. The dome seemed to be made of a single piece of perfectly formed glass. Outside, the sky was icy blue. Only a handful of wispy white clouds marred the otherwise uniform expanse. Glitch got the distinct impression he was inside a giant snow globe. It wouldn't have surprised him if the room had suddenly been picked up and shaken.

There was a low rumbling from somewhere beneath the room, and Glitch tensed. But no giant hands reached out of that near-perfect sky. Nor did the glass shatter, slicing them to shreds, which was the other disaster scenario Glitch's imagination conjured up.

The room was filled with dozens of identical machines set out in a grid. Each one was about fifteen feet high and comprised of a metallic sphere resting on a cylindrical plinth. Thick metal cables sprouted from each of the spheres, weaving around each other and the plinth to create a nest-like structure before vanishing into the floor. A quiet humming filled the room, and the faint smell of ozone hung in the air.

But Zheng and Anderson weren't looking at the machines. They'd moved to the edge of the room and were looking through the dome. As soon as Glitch joined them, he understood why.

The dome was located on top of a building in the center of a huge city. Hundreds, probably thousands of buildings stretched out before them, and each building was unique. Some were simple metal blocks, polished to a mirror sheen or roughly textured. Others were egg shaped or spherical. Still more were seemingly random clusters of geometric blocks, cubes, cylinders, and pyramids.

There seemed to be no organization to the structures, but roads ran between them. Or maybe they were paths—it was difficult to tell from so high up. There was movement along them—tiny ants that could be people or vehicles or actual ants.

Most of the buildings were solid, but a few appeared to be made of scaffolding. One of the nearest looked like a giant spiral staircase over thirty feet wide with steps that were at least two floors deep.

Six other domed buildings lay dotted around the city, seemingly identical to the one they were in. They were the tallest buildings by far, at least four times the height of any of the others. The body of each one was a simple cylinder, and the dome sat on a flat disk on top. The cylinders were about a third of the width of the disk, and there were no markings along their lengths, no windows or elevators.

Glitch could barely believe what he was seeing. "Maybe we're on Rama?"

"Pardon?" asked Anderson. She was in awe of the sight stretched out before them, and she didn't look at Glitch when she spoke.

"Rama. It's a spaceship from a book by Arthur C. Clarke. There's a mysterious city in it a bit like this one."

"What happens?"

"Nothing much, really," said Glitch.

Zheng tutted, and Glitch suddenly wished he hadn't brought it up.

At the far edge of the city, so distant they were barely visible, stood a range of orange-red mountains. A few shredded clouds clung to the tops of the jagged peaks, but there was no sign of snow. The view of the mountains was slightly distorted. At first Glitch assumed it was some sort of heat haze, but then there was a burst of bright light off to his left. The light flared again in a different place.

Zheng had seen it too. She gasped. "It's an energy field." She shook her head.

A dark shape swept in front of them, some sort of bird or a drone; it was gone too quickly to tell for sure. Glitch delicately tapped the dome. It rang slightly, an almost musical sound.

"It is secure."

It was Kalith. She was standing behind them as they took in the remarkable view.

"It's... incredible," said Zheng. "This is your capital?"

"Do not understand."

"Your main city. Where your leaders live."

"Only city."

Zheng's eyes widened in surprise. "There's only one Invisitude city?"

"Yes. Very few Invisitude."

"Are there other races?" said Glitch. His thoughts were on his essay. He hadn't included energy beings in it, but he'd covered most of the standard aliens—grays, little green men, humanoids with pointy ears.

"Yes," said Kalith. "There are many."

"But you are the primary species?" asked Doctor Zheng.

"Do not understand."

"The most intelligent, the most advanced."

"Yes."

Light flashed on the street far below them as sunlight caught something silver. The ground began to shake. Glitch pressed his hand against the dome to steady himself. The glass was warm. The earthquake lasted a full minute. There was a soft thump, and a thin pillar of smoke rose from one of the other domed buildings.

Kalith stared at it then turned back to Zheng. "Please. Time is limited."

Zheng glared at Glitch as though he was the one who had been causing the delay. He felt a wave of indignation but blushed anyway.

"I'm sorry," said Zheng. Her voice cracked a little.

Anderson moved toward her, a look of concern on her face.

Zheng frowned and gave a slight shake of her head. "How can we help?"

Kalith bowed slightly then turned and swept her hand in an arc, gesturing toward the machines filling the room. "This is geogrid. Network of geons. Harnesses gravitational energy. Stabilizes core. Maintains planet integrity."

Zheng looked around the room. Glitch wouldn't have thought it was possible for her to look more excited, but her face filled with wonder. It reminded Glitch of his five-year-old nephew opening presents on Christmas morning.

"This geogrid holds the planet together?" asked Zheng. "That is incredible. Just incredible."

"Yes," said Kalith. "There are limits. Instability is increasing. Exceeding geogrid capacity. Collapse is inevitable."

A look of genuine sadness flickered across Zheng's face. "But, Kalith, Earth does not have this level of technology." She gave a snort of contempt. "We can barely keep our own planet in one piece. How can we possibly help you?"

"We need sanctuary."

Now it was Anderson's turn to look incredulous. "Sanctuary? You want to come to Earth?"

Kalith bowed her head. "Yes."

"I'm sorr—"

"Yes," said Zheng. Anderson opened her mouth to object, but Zheng ignored her. "We will provide whatever assistance we can to you and your people."

"Thank you."

"I think what Doctor Zheng meant to say," said Anderson, her eyes fixed on Zheng, "is that we'll discuss your situation with the appropriate authorities. I'm sure Earth will gladly provide whatever assistance it can."

"I understand," said Kalith.

"But, Captain," said Zheng, her hands stabbing the air, emphasizing each word. "The technology here is incredible. The benefits of the knowledge the Invisitude could bring would be immense. We can't just let that opportunity pass us by."

Without moving, Anderson seemed to grow slightly. Her presence in the room became stronger, as though she'd turned on her authority boosters. Glitch could suddenly see how she'd become captain.

When she spoke, her voice was calm, quiet, and filled with determination. "That is true, Doctor Zheng. We'll talk to the government about the situation here."

At the mention of the government, Zheng gave a dismissive snort. Glitch couldn't disagree with Zheng's assessment of the idea.

"We *will* talk to them," continued Anderson, "but we do not have the authority to commit to more than that."

Doctor Zheng started to protest, but Anderson raised her eyebrows, and the doctor's voice trailed off.

Anderson waited until it was clear Doctor Zheng wasn't going to object further, then she turned back to Kalith. "How much longer can the geogrid keep the planet in one piece?"

"Three Earth weeks. At best."

"And at worst?"

"One Earth week."

Glitch looked at Zheng. That wasn't a lot of time to cut through government bureaucracy to solve even a simple problem, and what to do with a group of alien refugees was far from simple.

"We don't have very long," said Doctor Zheng, "but I'm sure we can find a way to help you." She looked toward Anderson as though daring the captain to contradict her.

A shadow moved across the corner of Glitch's vision. Before he could mention it to Anderson, the man in the black suit, John Smith, walked out from behind one of the geons. Glitch saw no sign of his gun, but Smith was holding a sleek silver object and wearing a smug smile.

"You're right, Doctor Zheng." Smith's voice was filled with contempt, and he almost spat her name. "That isn't much time, and unfortunately things are about to get a lot worse."

The group stared at Smith, his surprise arrival and the apparently limitless depths of his confidence leaving Glitch speechless, along with everyone else.

It was Anderson who eventually broke the silence. "How exactly are things going to get worse?"

Smith held out his arm, the silver object hanging between his finger and thumb. He waggled his hand, and sunlight glinted off the metal. "Clicky, clicky. Boomy, boomy."

Glitch saw Anderson's eyes darting around the room. She caught sight of something she didn't like, and her jaw clenched. Glitch followed her gaze and found the source of her anger. Three of the geons had silver packages attached to them. The packages were shaped like egg boxes designed to hold seven eggs. There were no blinking lights, no obvious wires, no big red buttons, but it wasn't much of a leap of logic to assume they were explosives.

Kalith moved forward, and as she did so, she grew taller and wider, more imposing. "You know him?"

"Not exactly," said Zheng. "He brought me here against my will and destroyed the gateway on Earth."

"Gateway is... destroyed?"

Smith laughed. "Yes, Ms. Kalith. Gateway is destroyed.

Plan is failure. Planet will collapse."

Kalith advanced toward Smith again. Flashes of red flickered through her body.

"Ah, ah, ah!" said Smith, waving the metallic object.

Kalith tilted her head but continued moving.

"He wants you to stop," said Anderson. "He's rigged explosives to some of those machines."

Kalith stopped moving, but more red flickered through her body.

"You're such a smart cookie, Ms. Anderson," said Smith. "I guess that's how you got to be captain so quickly. Or was it Daddy's influence?"

Anderson pursed her lips. "What do you want?"

"Oh, the usual. World peace, unlimited wealth, that sort of thing." Smith gave Anderson a huge, toothy grin. "Actually, I don't want anything."

Smith squeezed the metal object, and it changed color from silver to red.

The lights on the explosives began to blink.

CHAPTER SEVEN
The Saboteur Strikes

Doctor Zheng has been placed inside an electrified cage by John Smith. With the help of Kalith, an alien being made entirely of energy, Glitch and Captain Anderson free Zheng. Kalith explains that the planet her people, the Invisitude, inhabit is collapsing. She opened a gateway to Earth in the hope that the human race might be able to provide sanctuary for the Invisitude. She takes the humans to a domed building overlooking the Invisitude city, where they are surprised by John Smith, who has attached explosives to part of the geogrid—the technology that is preventing the planet from collapsing.

Captain Anderson pursed her lips. "What do you want?"

"Oh, the usual. World peace, unlimited wealth, that sort of thing," said Smith. He gave Anderson a huge, toothy grin. "Actually, I don't want anything."

Smith squeezed the sleek metal object. It changed color from silver to red.

The lights on the explosives began to blink.

Anderson moved toward the machines, but Glitch grabbed her arm.

"No!" he shouted. He dragged her backward, toward the entrance to the room.

Zheng had already taken cover behind one of the other machines. She was too far from the door to risk making a break for it. Kalith didn't move. Either she hadn't realized what Smith had done, or she couldn't quite believe he'd done it.

Smith darted behind the machinery, moving away from the door. Surely that meant he'd given himself a few minutes to escape?

He hadn't.

The first explosion tore apart the side of the machine farthest from Glitch and Anderson. Metal screamed as it was ripped into dozens of razor-sharp fragments and flung across the room. Glitch turned away, trying to cover himself and Captain Anderson with his arms. He flinched as shards of metal bounced past, ricocheting off the metal floor. A sheet of metal spun by, a lethal Frisbee whistling past Glitch's head. The room grew warm, and the hairs on the back of his neck stood up. Smoke filled the air as flames took hold of the machine's carcass.

There was another explosion, the sound oddly muffled. Fresh lumps of metal, some of them burning, bounced around them. A chunk about the size of Glitch's hand slammed into the dome covering the room and left a black scorch mark across its surface. Thick gray smoke billowed across the room, blocking the view of the city. Glitch pressed his hand over his mouth to protect himself from the smoke, but the air around him was clear, if a little metallic.

The third explosion was the closest, and Glitch was sure that this time, they'd be hit. But despite them being less than twenty feet away and in the direct path of the explosion, none of the debris scattered about the room hit them.

As the rain of debris slowed, Glitch looked back toward the sites of the explosions. His view was blocked by Kalith. At least, he thought it was her.

She stood between Glitch and Anderson and the three machines that Smith's explosives had destroyed. But she'd changed shape. Her legs had merged into one solid block and, along with her body, had spread out, creating a wall between them and the explosions. Debris littered the floor in front of Kalith where it had hit her and bounced off. Glitch shuddered at the thought of what those jagged fragments would have done to them if Kalith hadn't been there.

With a pop, the nearest machine emitted a shower of sparks. The tubes and cables had been torn free, and a thick, brown, soup-like substance was leaking steadily from the remains. The machines themselves had been reduced to twisted wrecks, blackened and burned. Whatever was in those devices had packed a punch.

"Are you okay?" said Glitch.

"Yes," said Anderson. "You?"

"I… think so. Thanks to Kalith."

"Doctor? Are you okay?" called Anderson.

Zheng peeked her head around the corner of the geon she was hiding behind and nodded. When she saw how Kalith had transformed, her caution vanished. She stood and almost ran across the room to join Anderson and Glitch. Kalith was returning to her humanoid form.

Zheng stood in front of her with a look of astonishment on her face. "That was incredible."

Kalith bowed slightly. "I have duty. To protect guests."

"Thank you," said Anderson. She was looking around the room, peering through the smoke.

"Any sign of Smith?" asked Glitch.

Anderson shook her head.

Kalith crossed the room and examined the nearest machine. Tendrils of electricity leaped from her hands to the wreckage. There was a crack, and a thin pillar of black smoke drifted up from the back of the machine. The ground shuddered, and metal groaned somewhere beneath the floor.

"You must go," said Kalith.

"But we can help with repairs," said Zheng.

"You must go," repeated Kalith. There was an urgency to her voice that made Glitch nervous.

A desperate look came over Zheng's face, but Anderson raised her hand. "Why?"

Before Kalith could reply, the door they'd come through opened, and two Invisitude entered the room. They were bigger than Kalith, broader, and they were a deep red color. They took up positions on either side of the door. Kalith positioned herself between the humans and the gateway but didn't speak.

A third Invisitude came through the door.

Kalith bowed slightly. "Councilor Kurtz."

The new arrival, Kurtz, was smaller than Kalith and the red Invisitude and was a dark gray color.

"Well done, Kalith." Despite his small stature, Kurtz's voice was deep, ominous. He gestured toward the two red Invisitude. "Arrest them."

Anderson tensed as the red Invisitude moved forward.

"Wait," said Kalith. "They not responsible."

Kurtz raised his hand, halting the red Invisitude. "Explain."

"Another human. Destroy geogrid. Sabotage."

Red energy flickered through Kurtz. He looked at the humans, and Glitch felt the Invisitude's anger wash over him. It was a physical sensation so strong that Glitch thought it might trigger a heart attack.

"Humans work together," said Kurtz. "Attack Invisitude."

"No!" said Zheng. "We would never do that. That man does not represent Earth. Earth is peaceful."

Kurtz gave a derisive snort. "Earth not peaceful."

Glitch thought Kurtz might have a point but kept his mouth shut. Zheng stepped toward Kurtz. He backed away, and the two red Invisitude moved to intercept her.

Anderson grabbed Zheng's shoulder, pulling her away. "Doctor."

The red Invisitude stopped just in front of Kurtz, protecting him.

"Please," said Anderson, "the doctor is right. We're not responsible for the explosions. We can help you find the man who did this."

"No," said Kurtz. "Humans are guilty."

"Where is proof?" said Kalith.

Kurtz gestured toward the wreckage of the geogrid. "It is clear. Humans are guilty."

The ground shuddered, and the building lurched.

"Maybe we should discuss this somewhere else?" said Glitch.

"Humans are guilty," said Kurtz. "Sentence is passed."

"What?" said Glitch.

Anderson reached toward her belt, where her gun would be if she were armed. "What's the sentence?"

"No authority, Councilor," said Kalith.

More red flashed through Kurtz. "I have authority. Situation is clear. Sentence is passed. Sentence is death."

CHAPTER EIGHT
Sentenced to Death

John Smith triggers an explosion, destroying part of the geogrid, a network of machines that maintain the planet's stability. Doctor Zheng manages to take cover, but Glitch and Captain Anderson are caught in the explosion. The Invisitude, Kalith, creates a barrier that protects them both from the explosion. In the chaos, Smith escapes.

Another Invisitude, Councilor Kurtz, arrives, accompanied by two red Invisitude—guards. Kurtz believes that Glitch, Anderson, and Zheng are working with Smith and are responsible for the attack on the geogrid.

"Humans are guilty," said Kurtz. "Sentence is passed."

"What?" said Glitch.

Anderson reached toward her belt, where her gun would be if she were armed. "What's the sentence?"

"No authority, Councilor," said Kalith.

A flash of red rippled through Kurtz. "I have authority. Situation is clear. Sentence is passed. Sentence is death."

Kalith swept toward Kurtz. "No."

Kurtz gestured toward the two red guards, and they advanced on Kalith. Kalith raised her arms, and the lightning bolts Glitch had secretly been expecting finally made an appearance.

Electricity burst from Kalith's right hand. It leapt across the room and hit the nearest guard. The moment it touched the Invisitude, it spread out, wrapping around the Invisitude's body and encasing it in a cage of blue-white energy. The energy crackled and popped, and the air filled with the smell of burning metal. The red Invisitude fell back.

Kalith twisted and pointed at the back of the room. "Go. Now."

No one needed to be told twice. They turned and ran.

With a crackle, the smell of burning metal grew stronger. Kurtz shouted something unintelligible. Some animal instinct kicking in, Glitch ducked behind the nearest geon. The side of the machine exploded, sending more metal bouncing across the room.

"Careful!" shouted Kurtz.

Smoke filled the air again. It caught in Glitch's throat, and he coughed. Waving his hand in front of his face, he peered through the haze. He'd lost Anderson and Zheng.

Terrified they'd been hit by the Invisitude's attack, he shouted, "Captain? Doctor?"

"Over here."

It was Anderson's voice. As the smoke thinned, Glitch could just about make out a dark shadow across the room.

The shadow waved at him. Another machine exploded. Glitch ran, heading for the nearest cover, one of the undamaged geons.

As soon as he was in the open, he realized it was a mistake. He was exposed. The Invisitude would almost certainly be able to see through the smoke. He'd never been athletic, and now his lumbering form would be an easy target for the guards. It would only be a matter of seconds before he felt his nervous system frying, and his little jaunt to an alien planet would be over.

And then he was behind the next geon, nervous system intact. The shadow was closer, and Glitch could see it was Anderson. Zheng stood behind her. They'd found a door, and Zheng was running her fingers around the edge, trying to get it to open.

Electricity crackled again. Someone cried out, but it was too far away and in the opposite direction for it to be Anderson or Zheng. It had to be one of the guards. Or Kalith.

"Come on!" shouted Anderson.

Glitch ran to her. The geon nearest the door had been destroyed by one of Smith's blasts. Metal cables and piping lay draped around the machine like snakes or an octopus's limbs.

Zheng was still trying to open the exit. Just as in the lab, there was a metal plate mounted beside the door. Glitch reached past Zheng and confidently pressed his palm against the plate.

Nothing happened.

He pressed harder.

Nothing happened.

Zheng sighed and knocked Glitch's hand away. Glitch felt a flush of heat rush to his face. He watched Zheng run her hands over and around the door, searching for a catch that would open it. Behind them, Kurtz shouted orders to fan out and find the humans.

One of the cables hanging from the geon sparked and twitched. Glitch stared at it for a moment then took a deep breath and grabbed it. He squeezed his eyes shut, waiting for the electricity to kill him. When it didn't come, he pulled the cable toward the door panel. It stopped a couple of feet short. Glitch cursed and pulled at the cable. It shifted a couple of inches but still fell short.

The air crackled with electricity, and the wall beside Glitch exploded in a cloud of smoke. A chunk of metal caught him on the shoulder, and he yelled. Glitch winced as he followed the cable back to the machine. It was hooked around a torn chunk of the geon. Glitch unhooked the cable, pulled it over to the door, and pressed the exposed end into the metal plate. Sparks leapt from the end of the cable and something inside the wall whined, but the door stayed closed.

Glitch cursed again and jammed the cable harder against the plate. More sparks burst from the end of the cable. They landed on the back of Glitch's hand, leaving little red burns. This time, the door juddered open. Doctor Zheng almost fell through the opening.

"Look out!" screamed Anderson.

Glitch ducked. A ball of energy about twice the size of his head slammed into the wall beside the door. The impact tore a hole in the wall and scattered pieces of burnt metal across the ground. One of the chunks landed on Glitch's shoulder. He swatted it away, but not before it had burned a hole through his jacket.

Anderson grabbed Glitch and dragged him through the opening just before the door slid shut again. They were standing in a metal corridor almost identical to the one Kalith had taken them down when they'd first arrived—the same metal walls, the same harsh lights. But there were no other doors nearby. In either direction, the corridor continued thirty feet or so and ended in a T-junction.

There was a heavy thump as something hit the door behind them.

"This way!" shouted Zheng. She was already twenty feet down the corridor and almost at the nearest T-junction.

Glitch and Anderson ran after her. The corridors leading away from the junction were empty, just long expanses of silver metal ending in two more T-junctions.

"Left?" asked Glitch.

Anderson nodded. They ran down the corridor. Anderson reached the next junction first.

"There," said Glitch, pointing toward a circular hatch in the wall about halfway down the right-hand corridor. "Come on."

He ran to the door, Anderson and Zheng close behind. Two silver panels were embedded in the wall on either side of the door. Glitch pressed the right-hand one. The door clicked and made a high-pitched beep but didn't open.

"Try the other one," said Zheng.

Glitch felt a flash of anger. He wasn't an idiot. He pressed the second panel. With another click and an even higher-pitched beep, the door slid into the floor. It moved maddeningly slowly. Glitch pushed the door down, trying to speed it up, but the door was determined to take its own sweet time.

A bolt of energy flew down the corridor, so close that Glitch could smell the air burning.

The hatch was almost completely open; certainly there was enough room to get through it. But Glitch hesitated. The passage beyond quickly disappeared into darkness, and the air stank of rotting food and worse. "It smells bad in there."

"Get in there," said Anderson. "I don't care what you smell." She nudged Glitch toward the opening with her foot.

More scared of looking like a coward than of whatever olfactory delights they'd find inside the tunnel, Glitch clambered through the hatch. His left foot caught on the edge of the door, slowing him down and earning him a sigh from Doctor Zheng.

"Hurry, Dwayne," she said. She was already starting to annoy him.

Glitch glared at her and ducked inside. The space was narrow, and he had to crawl on his hands and knees. He checked behind him, managing to make out Zheng and

Anderson before the hatch slid closed, plunging the tunnel into darkness. The floor and walls were slick, and he'd barely made it ten feet before his hand landed on something thick and viscous. Lifting his hand and flicking away the substance, Glitch fought down the urge to throw up.

"Are you okay?" hissed Anderson.

Glitch nodded and realized she wouldn't be able to see him in the darkness. "Yes, but I don't want to think about what I just put my hand in."

"In that case," said Zheng, "perhaps you could get a move on before the Invisitude find us."

Fighting back a smart-ass response, Glitch crawled down the passage. He shuddered as unknown liquid seeped through the knees of his jeans. His eyes were beginning to adjust to the darkness. He couldn't see much more than dark shapes outlined against even darker walls, but there was clearly some light coming from somewhere. Even that minimal visibility helped boost Glitch's confidence, and he picked up the pace.

Which meant he didn't have time to react when the ground beneath him gave way, pitching him forward into an opening in the floor.

Glitch yelled as his shoulder hit metal, and he began sliding. He pressed his hands against the wall, trying to slow his progress. It worked at first, then the heat caused by the friction forced him to ease up. The chute shuddered as another earthquake hit. He heard Zheng and Anderson calling after him, their voices echoing off the metal walls.

He shouted a brief warning then reached the end of the chute.

Glitch flew through the air. He felt as if he was hanging there like some cartoon character, and as long as he didn't look down, he'd be fine. Then gravity caught hold of him, and he dropped.

He managed to land feet first but immediately fell onto his back. The impact sent a jarring pain up his spine, and he crumpled to the floor. He cried out, convinced he'd shattered his legs or at the very least crushed a couple of vertebrae.

Glitch lay there, his eyes squeezed shut while the pain dissipated. When he opened them again, he found himself in a cave made of the same red rock as the one they'd first arrived in. Maybe they'd ended up back at the gateway and they'd be able to go home again.

A quiet voice echoed through the cave, and it took Glitch a few seconds to work out that Anderson was calling to him down the chute.

"Are you okay?" she asked.

"I think so," he shouted. His voice echoed off the cave walls. The sound was uncomfortably loud.

Anderson asked the same question again, evidently unable to hear Glitch.

Glitch wiggled his toes. They moved, and he felt them inside his sneakers. If the dozens of TV doctors Glitch had grown up with were to be believed, that meant he hadn't managed to cripple himself. Slowly, Glitch rolled onto his side, hyperconscious of every twinge and ache as his body rebelled against the movement. Glitch pushed himself into a sitting position. The world swam, and a wave of nausea washed over him.

He closed his eyes until everything settled into its natural position. When he opened them again, he did so slowly, not wanting to trigger another round of dizziness. When he was confident he'd gotten all his internal organs back under control, he looked around. The cave was about forty feet square, and it looked man made. Or Invisitude made, he supposed.

It was filled with garbage. Rotting food, sheets of metal, cables, wire, and fragments of red rock lay scattered around. He was lucky he hadn't landed on anything sharp. The air was thick with the stench of rotting vegetables and other odors that he didn't want to place. The hole he'd fallen through was cut into the rock wall, about ten feet above the floor.

He checked again to make sure he hadn't broken anything and breathed a sigh of relief when he found he hadn't. Other than the chute, there were no obvious ways in or out of the room.

"Glitch! Can you hear me?" Anderson's voice was strained, filled with concern.

Glitch stood on his tiptoes and shouted into the chute, "Yes! I'm okay."

"Where are you?"

"I'm in a cave."

"Is it safe?" This time it was Doctor Zheng's voice.

Glitch looked around the cave at the garbage. There

were dozens of places something could hide. Who knew what had slithered down the garbage chute and crawled off into a corner to wait for unsuspecting intergalactic travelers?

"I think so," called Glitch. "But there's no way out."

Maybe Anderson hadn't heard that last bit, because she shouted, "We're coming down."

"Be careful! There's a ten-foot drop at the end."

There was no reply. Glitch stood near the chute, alternately standing beneath it so that he could catch Anderson and off to one side so that she didn't hit him. In the end, he elected to stay well clear and backed up against a nearby wall.

Anderson came through the chute in a controlled slide, and to Glitch at least, she seemed to float to the ground. When she hit the floor, she tucked her head and let her forward momentum carry her into a roll. She was standing and scanning the room for threats before Glitch had a chance to offer her his help.

Zheng's arrival was only marginally less athletic. Between them, the women left Glitch feeling clumsy and inadequate.

Thirty seconds after Zheng arrived, she walked over to Glitch and backhanded his shoulder. The blow wasn't hard, but it took him by surprise.

"What was that for?" he said with an indignant frown.

Zheng swept her arm around the room.

Glitch followed the motion. "And?"

"Do you see any exits?"

"No," said Glitch. "I tried to warn you."

Before Zheng could respond, Anderson stepped between them. "It's okay. There was no way we could go back. The Invisitude weren't giving us a lot of options. At least now we get some time to think."

Glitch was grateful for the intervention, but there was enough uncertainty in Anderson's voice that he was pretty sure she agreed with Zheng's assessment. He'd been an idiot. Now they'd probably starve to death in an Invisitude trash heap.

A metallic rattle came from a pile of garbage in one corner of the room. The pile shifted slightly, then a cube of coppery metal tumbled down the side. Zheng glared at Glitch, and he looked away. There was no sign of seams or other breaks in the rock walls, which raised the question of what happened to all the garbage as the room filled up.

"At least the walls aren't going to start closing in," said Glitch.

A low rumble rolled through the ground. A scattering of dust drifted down from the ceiling. Glitch watched the walls nervously, suddenly concerned he'd spoken too soon. The noise died down. The room stopped shaking.

"So any ideas how we get out of here, *Dwayne*?" Zheng stressed his name, lacing the word with just a dash of contempt.

Glitch felt his face grow hot. He turned away and examined a nearby pile of rotting food. Grabbing a metal pipe, he poked at the soggy mass as though it might reveal some hitherto-unseen trapdoor. In fact, that wasn't such a stupid idea. "Maybe there's a trapdoor."

Zheng looked dubious, but Anderson evidently agreed with him. "All this garbage has to go somewhere eventually. See if you can find any openings, even something small."

Glitch felt a small flash of probably unwarranted pride. He poked away at the food, using the pipe to reveal the rock beneath. There was no trapdoor, just the same red rock they'd found everywhere else.

Glitch moved around the room, checking the floor with the pipe. In places, the rock was slick with rotten food, but for the most part, it was hard and dry. A dozen or so cracks cut across the floor, some of them deep enough to hide parcels of rancid vegetable matter. Glitch poked at one of the cracks. It was shallow, but Glitch's prodding was enough to unleash a wave of noxious gas trapped inside.

Anderson and Zheng's investigation was equally fruitless. All that remained was the pile of metal, plastic, and cloth that had shifted position earlier. Glitch stood next to it, clutching the metal pipe in a hand that was suddenly sweating. Anderson moved to take the pipe, but before she could, Glitch stepped forward and began pushing aside the pile of garbage.

Unlike with the decaying food, there was no real reason he shouldn't use his hands, but if something was lurking beneath the metal, he didn't want his exposed skin anywhere near it. Glitch dug around in the pile for several minutes, alert to signs of life as well as a potential exit. He found neither.

Eventually he stepped back from the garbage pile. "Nothing under there, either."

Doctor Zheng had already given up on Glitch's investigation and was standing beneath the chute. "Maybe we could climb back up."

"Two of us, maybe," said Anderson, "if the third one gave them a lift up, but the last person would be stuck."

Glitch suspected Zheng would quite happily nominate him as the sacrificial lamb. "Was there any rope? In the piles, I mean."

Zheng shook her head.

"I didn't see any," said Anderson. "In any case, that just gets us back into the hands of the Invisitude. I'd like to avoid that if we can."

Glitch looked around at the walls. They were clearly handmade, but the work was rough. The rock was uneven, and like the floor, there were a few cracks. "Maybe there's a hidden switch."

"That sounds a bit *Scooby Doo*," said Zheng.

Glitch doubted Zheng had ever actually watched that show, but he ignored her and looked at Anderson instead.

"It's worth a try," she said.

The three of them stopped talking and wandered around the room, examining the walls instead. Glitch pressed his hands against the cold rock. Despite the fact it had been his idea, he doubted they'd find anything. He was halfway around the room when the wall actually did move. It didn't swing open to reveal an exit, but it shifted beneath his hands.

He pressed harder against the wall, and it moved again. It was subtle, but he felt it give. "Err… Captain Anderson… Doctor Zheng. There's something here."

"What?" said the doctor, peering at the wall over his shoulder.

"The wall—it moves when I press against it."

The doctor seemed skeptical, but when she pressed her own hand against the rock, her eyes widened in surprise. As she pulled her hand away, a grinding sound came from somewhere deep in the wall.

Glitch stepped back, wondering if they really had found a secret passage. A couple of lumps of rock broke free from the wall and dropped to the floor, accompanied by a smattering of dust. Then the wall bulged. Two eyes blinked into existence.

Glitch smiled. "Fido."

As more rock fell away, it revealed an angular, battered face with a deep crack running down its right side like a scar.

Glitch's smile vanished. "Not Fido."

"Get back," said Anderson, grabbing Glitch's shoulder when he hesitated.

They retreated across the cavern as the creature pulled itself from the wall. Chunks of rock crumbled to the ground around its feet. It was bigger than Fido, well over nine feet tall and much broader. Its arms were thick and heavy, its hands clenched into two battered, scarred fists. The creature rolled its shoulders from side to side like a wet dog shaking itself. More fragments of rock scattered across the ground. It leaned forward and roared—a deep, gravelly sound that echoed off the walls. Its mouth was filled with teeth, short, stubby pillars of cracked rock.

The creature flicked its head, sniffing at the air, then stepped toward them.

CHAPTER NINE
The Beast from the Wall

Councilor Kurtz accuses Glitch, Anderson, and Zheng of sabotaging the geogrid that is maintaining the planet's stability. Kurtz sentences them to death, but Kalith protects them long enough for them to escape. They take cover in a small passageway but fall into a room filled with garbage. As they search for a way to escape, a rock creature crawls from the wall.

Glitch, Anderson, and Doctor Zheng retreated across the cavern as the creature pulled itself into the room. Chunks of rock fell from the wall, clustering around its feet.

It was bigger than Fido, well over nine feet tall and much broader. Its arms were like tree trunks, thick and heavy, and its hands were clenched into two battered, scarred fists. A deep crack ran down the right side of its face like a scar. The creature shook itself, dislodging more fragments of rock, then leaned forward and roared. The deep, gravelly sound echoed off the walls, and Glitch instinctively moved backward.

The creature flicked its head, sniffing at the air, then stepped toward them.

"What *is* that?" said Zheng. Her eyes were wide, a mixture of fear and curiosity on her face.

"Some sort of rock monster," said Glitch. "You know, an alien."

Zheng gave him a cold look. The scarred creature tilted its head and swept its gaze around the room as though making sure they couldn't escape. Then it took another lumbering step forward.

"If you really can kill people with your mind, now would be a good time," said Anderson, tipping her head toward Glitch's T-shirt.

He glared at the creature, eyes narrowed, teeth gritted, as though he was directing some sort of mind ray at it. Nothing happened. "Sorry, out of juice."

The creature roared again. Small lumps of rock fell from its mouth. It shook its head and walked forward, its right leg trailing behind it. As it moved, the creature tore chunks from the ground, sending lumps of red rock bouncing across the room and leaving deep gouges in the floor. One of the pieces of rock landed near Zheng. She picked it up and threw it. The rock bounced off the creature's head, and it let out another cry.

"Maybe if you stop trying so hard to annoy it, it'll get bored and wander off," said Glitch.

"Maybe if I feed you to it, it'll leave the two of us alone," said Zheng.

The creature took another step, and they backed away, edging ever closer to the wall.

"Any better ideas for dealing with Scarface, Captain?" said Glitch.

"If I think of any, I'll let you know."

The ground shuddered, and a narrow crack appeared in the floor, zigzagging away from the creature toward the back of the cave. Scarface hesitated, twisting its head to the right. It roared again, the noise quieter this time but no less threatening. The cry seemed directed toward an uneven patch of rock in the wall opposite it.

Something responded. A soft growl. The creature let out another roar as the wall cracked and distorted. A second rock creature broke into the room. The newcomer was smaller, leaner. It looked at Glitch and smiled. It was Fido.

Fido turned to Scarface and snarled. He charged across the room and slammed into Scarface. There was a loud crack as they collided, sending fragments of rock bouncing across the room. Scarface gave a deep-throated scream and swung its arm at Fido's head, but while it was bigger and stronger than Fido, Scarface was slower. Fido shifted, ducking out of the way. The heavy fist swung harmlessly through the air.

Fido darted forward, grabbing Scarface around the waist and pushing it back. The creatures fell over. Fresh cracks snaked across the ground. Glitch leapt backward, away from the fight and the unstable ground.

Scarface tried to roll over and pin Fido to the floor, but

Fido was too quick. He released his grip, rolled to the right, and stood, leaping out of reach of the other creature's flailing fists. Scarface slowly pulled itself into a crouch and watched warily as Fido circled it. A new crack ran down Scarface's left arm, but otherwise it seemed unharmed.

Glitch took advantage of the lull to move around the room and join Zheng and Anderson. The three of them backed away from the battling creatures and pressed themselves against the wall. The thought that there might be a third rock creature, one as aggressive as Scarface, flickered through Glitch's mind. Before it could take root in his imagination, he quashed the image of giant rock hands reaching out of the wall to crush his skull. Fido feinted, lunging forward. The scarred creature reared backward, swinging its right arm upward but missing. Fido slammed into Scarface's left shoulder. There was a brittle snapping sound as the creature's arm twisted back.

Fido wrapped his arm around Scarface's head, his fingers digging into the creature's cheek. Scarface screamed in agony. It bucked and twisted, trying to throw off Fido.

Fido pulled, twisting the creature's head sideways. Rock shattered, and the side of Scarface's head broke away. Fido threw it across the room then swung a fist. The impact made a sickening crunch. Fragments of rock skittered across the floor as Scarface's head shattered into hundreds of pieces.

Fido let go of Scarface and leapt back. Minus a head, Scarface fell backward onto the floor. The creature lay there for a second before dissolving into the ground like melting ice. Glitch stared at the floor where the creature had vanished then looked hurriedly around the room, watching for signs of movement in the walls. Something rumbled—rock grinding against rock somewhere beneath their feet—but otherwise everything was still.

Fido let out a snort. He turned and walked toward Glitch. He was limping, favoring his right leg. A narrow fissure ran down its length, damage from the fight, but as he got nearer, the fissure closed up until it was a barely visible scratch and he was walking normally again.

"Thank you," said Glitch.

Glitch couldn't tell whether Fido could understand him, but the creature gave a slight grunt and nodded. That was good enough.

Doctor Zheng eyed the patch of floor where Scarface had fallen. "Do you think that... thing will be back?"

"I'd rather not stay around to find out," said Anderson.

Zheng frowned and turned her attention to Fido. "These things really are quite remarkable. We should take the time to examine them while we can."

Before Glitch or Anderson could reply, there was another rumble, louder this time, and the ground shuddered. Glitch pressed his hand against the wall to steady himself, and Fido smiled. He reached out, mirroring Glitch's movement but letting his hand merge with the rock. It looked as if his arm was the branch of a red rock tree growing out of the wall. Glitch laughed and winked at Fido. Fido's smile grew into a broad grin, and he winked back. He laughed and pulled his arm from the wall, depositing a few fresh shards of rock on the floor.

The ground shook again. A lump of rock fell from the ceiling in the middle of the room and crashed into the floor. There was a sharp cracking sound, and one of the fissures created by the fighting rock creatures widened, snaking across the ground toward Glitch.

"Look out," screamed Glitch.

The ground beneath them buckled and twisted. A couple of feet away, a broad chunk of the floor collapsed, and a blast of heat washed over them. Glitch stepped backward as another piece of rock, much bigger than the first, collapsed.

Steam billowed from the opening in the floor, and Doctor Zheng gasped. Beneath the room was a tunnel filled with a slow-moving river of hissing, boiling liquid. The air was filled with a thick, sulfurous smell. Glitch pressed his hand over his mouth, his eyes watering.

More fissures opened, zigzagging across the ground. Glitch felt the floor beneath his feet give way. He was pitched forward, his stomach lurching. He dropped to his knees, clinging desperately to the rock as it plummeted toward the boiling liquid. Behind him, someone screamed.

As the slab of rock hit the liquid, Glitch closed his eyes, waiting for a wave of scalding whatever-it-was to wash over him. There was a hissing sound and a blast of intense heat but nothing more. He opened his eyes. The rock had righted itself on the surface and was floating. A viscous liquid splashed onto the edges of the slab, hissing and spitting as it hit the dusty surface. Glitch backed away to the middle of his makeshift raft.

The boiling river flowed through a narrow, winding tunnel. The walls were ragged and worn, and for a moment, Glitch considered trying to jump off the rock. Then he realized all he'd be able to do was cling there until his arms gave out and he fell into the scalding liquid, and he thought better of it.

Glitch looked back toward the opening he'd fallen through. The floor of the cave was almost completely gone, the last few pieces just crumbling away and dropping into the liquid. He peered through the steam, trying to find Anderson and Doctor Zheng, but there was no sign of either of them. Or of Fido.

His slab of rock lurched forward as it caught on something beneath the surface of the river. Glitch clutched at the rock, fingers scrabbling for purchase. There was a grinding sound as the rock broke free, righting itself as it continued its journey.

The heat was almost unbearable. Sweat poured down Glitch's back and into his eyes as his body fought to cool itself. Steam and smoke filled the air, catching in his throat and making him cough.

The rock collided with the edge of the tunnel. It twisted sideways, slowly rotating as the river carried him away from the cave.

Glitch scanned the walls, searching desperately for a drier tunnel or even just a ledge—some way out of the mess he was in. It was beginning to look as though death by rock monster would have been a better way to go. Glitch coughed. Every breath he took was agony as the sulfur burned his throat and lungs.

A few feet ahead, the river vanished into a wall of steam. Glitch heard the liquid hissing and spitting. The slab lurched again, and more liquid splashed over the side. Glitch wiped at the sweat pouring down his forehead. It splashed into his eyes. His head was pounding, and he felt himself waver. Blackness tugged at him, tempting him. He could just lie back and let it take him. He could sleep through his death.

The steam was so thick that he could barely see the rock he was riding on. The air was full of hissing and cracking sounds, and Glitch felt the rock beneath his hands growing hotter and hotter. The slab seemed to be moving faster, gathering speed as it traveled through the steam. There was a jolt, and the rock spun sideways then tipped violently forward. The steam thinned for a moment. The river was carrying Glitch toward the edge of a waterfall.

Glitch swore as he was carried over the top of a waterfall. He slid forward, his fingers scrabbling against the rock as it fell toward a lake of bubbling, roiling liquid. Steam billowed around him, hot against his arms and face. The rock flipped forward, and his fingers slipped.

Glitch fell backward toward the scalding liquid.

CHAPTER TEN
Steamed Glitch

Trapped inside a garbage disposal room, Glitch, Captain Anderson, and Doctor Zheng are attacked by a rock creature. Fido comes to their aid and defeats the much larger creature. Damage caused by their battle makes the floor of the room collapse. With Anderson and Zheng missing, Glitch finds himself floating down a river of sulfurous, boiling liquid on a slab of rock.

The steam billowing around the rock was so thick that Glitch could barely see his hand in front of his face. The rock beneath his feet grew hotter and hotter, cracking as it expanded. It was accelerating, rushing Glitch toward who knew what. He heard a roaring sound, rapidly increasing in volume.

The rock hit something, spinning sideways. It tipped forward, and the steam thinned for a moment, revealing a waterfall. Glitch swore as the rock tipped over its edge.

Glitch slipped forward, his fingers clutching at the rock

as it plummeted toward the lake of boiling liquid below. Glitch hit a patch of steam, the moisture hot against his arms and face. The rock flipped forward, his fingers slipped, and he fell backward toward the scalding liquid.

Something grabbed Glitch's wrist, yanking him upward. The slab of rock fell past him and disappeared into the writhing waters below.

Glitch looked up. A long, thin arm made of rock poked out of the steam, four chunky fingers wrapped around Glitch's wrist. His shoulder screamed in agony as he was dragged past the cascading liquid. The smell caught in Glitch's throat, threatening to choke him, but still, relief wrapped its comforting arms around him.

Fido came into view. He was hanging from the ceiling, a look of intense concentration on his face. Just below him was a ledge running along the side of the tunnel. Anderson and Zheng were standing on it, backs pressed against the wall.

The ceiling shook. Glitch felt Fido's grip loosen. He grabbed at Fido's wrist, clinging on for dear life. Carrot-shaped pieces of rock fell from the ceiling. One of them hit Glitch, bouncing off his knee and sending a wave of pain up his leg. He moaned. It felt as though his shoulder would tear itself loose, and the ledge seemed a thousand miles away. Far farther than the deadly liquid beneath him.

Fido swung Glitch sideways. Glitch closed his eyes. For a moment, he thought Fido would fling him onto the ledge, Gimli style. Then he felt firm rock beneath his feet and the reassuring hands of Captain Anderson pulling him to safety. He knelt, collapsing to the ground in relief as soon as Fido let go of his wrist.

Glitch sat there, trying to slow his heart before it tore loose from his chest. Fido's rocky arm disappeared into the wall, leaving just his face staring down at Glitch. Glitch nodded his appreciation, eliciting a broad smile from Fido before his face also disappeared into the rock.

"Are you okay?" said Anderson, frowning at Glitch.

He hesitated, taking a deep breath and silently checking off limbs and organs before nodding. "It's just like Disneyland. A hot, deadly Disneyland. Without the mascots. Or the lines."

"He's okay," said Anderson to the doctor.

Zheng forced a smile. Glitch leaned back against the wall and took a deep breath, instantly regretting it. The sulfur smell wasn't as strong here, but it was still uncomfortable.

"So," he said, coughing, "where do we go from here?"

"The ledge seems solid enough to survive the earthquakes, but we need to get moving."

There was a soft rumbling, and the wall next to Glitch bulged outward until Fido's face appeared. He stepped onto the ledge and bent down, peering at Glitch with a childlike look of concern. Fido tilted his head and raised his heavy eyebrows.

Glitch gave a thumbs-up, hoping that was the universal sign for "Everything's good, feel free to save my life again in the future."

Fido straightened up, a broad grin spreading across his face. He raised one blocky hand and stared at it until it transformed into an approximation of a thumbs-up. Glitch smiled and nodded.

Steam hissed, and a column of liquid rose from the river like a fountain. Glitch pulled back as a wave of heat hit him. Fido laughed and kicked a few pebbles over the edge and into the river.

"Glitch, we need to get out of here," said Anderson.

Glitch waved at Fido. Once he was sure he had Fido's full, determinedly focused attention, Glitch pointed at himself, then to the left and right. "Which way?" He spoke slowly and loudly, as though he was talking to his senile grandfather.

Fido tensed, his eyes growing wide with excitement. He looked right then snapped his head left. He smiled slyly.

"No," said Glitch, shaking his head firmly. "I'm not playing."

Fido frowned and tilted his head, looking for all the world like a confused puppy. Glitch pointed at himself again then jabbed his fingers left and right. Another column of superheated liquid rose up, splattering the ceiling and splashing them with a few hot beads of liquid. Glitch motioned toward the river then tipped his head back, closed his eyes, and stuck out his tongue.

"What are you doing?" said Anderson.

"I'm playing dead," said Glitch around his tongue.

Anderson shook her head. "Come on." Anderson

began walking along the ledge, moving back up the river the way they'd come.

Fido ran up the wall, parkour style, past Anderson and onto the ledge in front of her. His face broke into a huge, ragged grin. He walked backward along the ledge in front of Anderson, matching her every step.

Glitch shook his head in mock despair and stood. "After you, Doctor Zheng."

The doctor looked nervously over the edge toward the boiling liquid then carefully skirted her way around Glitch. She followed Anderson, her hands clutching at the rough wall. Glitch let her get ahead a little way but stayed close enough that he might be able to catch her if she fell.

In places, the ledge was barely wide enough for them to pass, and they were forced to cling to the wall and shuffle sideways, trying not to think of the lethal river a few feet beneath them.

Eventually the ledge petered out almost completely, narrowing to a tiny strip barely two inches wide. Fido just continued walking, stepping into the wall, his feet merging with the rock to support his weight. After a few paces, he realized he wasn't being followed and stopped. He waved at them, beckoning them on. Anderson shook her head. She pointed toward the river hissing and spitting below. Fido shrugged and plodded back along the wall toward them.

Doctor Zheng leaned nervously around Anderson and looked at the sliver of rock the ledge had become. "We're stuck?"

"It looks like it," said Anderson. "We'll have to go back."

The doctor closed her eyes and let out a long breath. Glitch found himself doing the same. The doctor's anxiety was infectious.

"Maybe I could just wait here?" said the doctor.

"We'll take a quick break," said Anderson. "Try to relax, but don't breathe too deeply. The air's pretty bad."

Fido had attached himself to the wall nearby. He hung there, watching them expectantly. Glitch moved back to a wider section of the ledge and sat. The river hissed and spat. A wave of sulfur hit him, and he grimaced.

"You're looking a bit green," said Anderson, making Glitch jump. "Sorry," she said, smiling.

He shook his head. "The doctor may have the right idea. Maybe you and Fido should check out the other end of the ledge and come back and get us."

"How's your head?" said Anderson.

Glitch frowned. "A bit fuzzy but nothing compared to my last hangover."

"It's the air. There's oxygen here, but there's frak-knows-what-else mixed with it. If we're not careful, we'll pass out."

"Frak?"

"You're not the only science fiction geek on this planet, you know."

"The doctor likes science fiction?"

Anderson gave a laugh. "Nooooo, she's more of a science fact geek."

The doctor coughed. She was rubbing her temples, and her skin was pale.

"She doesn't look so hot. I mean, good. Not so good," said Glitch.

"No, she doesn't."

"We should go."

Anderson nodded, but as they moved to go back to the doctor, Glitch raised his hand. He was watching Fido. He was still clinging to the wall, but he'd apparently grown bored of watching them. He was systematically pushing his hand into the wall, pulling out a lump of red rock, and placing it back into the wall a few feet to his right. In the process, he was creating an opening.

"What's he doing?" said Anderson.

"I think he's digging us a way out."

Fido saw them watching him. He waved excitedly, calling them over. As they got closer, they could see the crevice was already a couple of feet deep and looked almost wide enough for Glitch to fit inside.

They watched as Fido worked. Encouraged by their attentiveness, he moved quicker, pulling more and more rock free until finally the back of the wall caved in. A pale light trickled through.

"It's a… way out…" said the doctor. Her voice was quiet, and she was leaning heavily against the wall.

More of the rock fell away, and Glitch felt a slight breeze against his cheek. The doctor coughed, a harsh rattle that quickly turned to retching. She leaned forward, her hand pressed against her chest. Anderson ran forward, caught the doctor as she slumped sideways, and lowered her gently toward the ground. The doctor lay there, eyes closed, her skin waxy.

Anderson pressed her hand against the doctor's neck. "We need to get her some air. Help me get her up."

Supporting her, Glitch and Anderson managed to get Zheng upright. She was smaller than both of them and fairly light, but it was difficult to maneuver her without one of them slipping off the ledge. After a couple of aborted attempts, they managed to half carry, half drag the doctor to the crevice.

Fido was still digging, but the opening was just wide enough for them to get through. Beyond it lay a cave lit by soft white light. Glitch felt cool, clean air filtering in from the other side. He dragged in two deep breaths, and the freshness brought home just how rancid the air they'd been breathing was.

As they drew near, Fido moved aside to let them into the gap. The edges of the opening were rough, and Anderson caught her jacket on a jagged piece of rock. With exaggerated care, Fido unhooked the jacket, then he tore away the offending chunk and threw it over his shoulder.

With almost painful slowness, Anderson and Glitch shuffled through the opening, the doctor's unconscious form dangling between them. They carried her a few feet into the cave and laid her carefully on the ground. Anderson slipped off her jacket and placed it under the doctor's head, then she checked Zheng's pulse again.

"Will she be okay?" said Glitch.

"I don't know for sure, but her pulse is pretty strong, and the air seems clear in here. That should help."

Glitch looked around. The cave was vast, but the ceiling was peppered with holes that let in broad pillars of light. The holes continued a few hundred feet to the left before stopping and letting the cave get swallowed up by shadows.

To the right, the floor rose at a steady incline. A faint glow rimmed the top of the rise. The walls and ceiling of the cave were made of the familiar red rock, but the floor was a darker red, and it was slick, like glass. In places the surface was cracked, and Glitch could see multiple layers. Different shades of rock formed as it had melted and solidified thousands of times.

Fido appeared, stepping out of the wall as usual, but he seemed nervous, almost scared. He looked around the cave then tentatively stepped across the slick floor, watching his feet carefully. He looked at Glitch and gave a halfhearted smile. He took another step, his right foot sliding on the glassy surface, then stood with a faintly terrified expression. Whatever powers gave Fido the ability to merge with rock clearly didn't extend to this new substance.

"Come on, Doctor. Think of all the exciting discoveries you're missing," said Anderson, her voice filled with worry.

"Is there anything I can do?" said Glitch.

Anderson tilted her head toward the slope. "Take a

look up there—see if there's some water or a way out. She needs fresh air more than anything. It's better here, but I'd still like to get out of these caves."

Glitch nodded and headed toward the slope. The slick surface made the ascent treacherous. He kept slipping, losing his balance, and twice he ended up thumping onto his backside. The second time he was pretty sure he heard Anderson laughing quietly to herself.

But about three quarters of the way up the slope, he reached a series of small holes in the floor. The edges were slick and difficult to grip, but they were just big enough to fit his hand into. The rock around the holes was warm, too hot to touch in some places. But there were dozens, perhaps hundreds of them, and they made the last thirty feet of the climb much easier.

A line of boulders lay scattered across the top of the hill, all of them made of the same slick rock as the slope. Glitch counted a dozen of various sizes, from bowling balls to one that was larger than Fido. From a distance, the rock seemed to glow with an inner light, but as he got closer, he saw the light was coming from beyond the crest of the hill.

Glitch grabbed one of the bigger boulders and hauled himself the last couple of feet up the slope. As he rounded the lump of rock, he stopped, his eyes growing wide. Glitch stood, staring for a minute, then called back down the slope. "Captain Anderson, you're going to want to see this."

"See what?"

Glitch turned back and stared at the planet hanging in the sky. "It's Earth."

CHAPTER ELEVEN
Visions of Earth

Glitch, Anderson, and Doctor Zheng are rescued from an underground river of boiling liquid by Fido, who places them on a narrow ledge. The air in the tunnel is toxic, and as they search for a way out, Doctor Zheng collapses. Fido breaks through the tunnel's wall, providing them with access to a cave and fresher air. As Anderson looks after an unconscious Doctor Zheng, Glitch climbs out of the cave.

Glitch dragged himself up the slope. The almost glass-like boulders running along its top seemed to glow, but as he got closer, he saw the light was coming from beyond the crest of the hill. He grabbed one of the boulders and hauled himself up the last couple of feet. He stopped, his eyes growing wide. Glitch stood transfixed for a minute then turned and called down the slope.

"Captain Anderson, you're going to want to see this."

"See what?"

Glitch turned back and stared at the planet hanging in

the sky. "It's Earth."

It was a familiar sight, a scene from hundreds of movies and documentaries and photographs, but still it took his breath away. No camera, no special effects company could come close to capturing the majesty of the blue planet. Glitch swallowed, his vision unexpectedly blurry.

There was movement beside him. "Wow," said Anderson.

"I thought you'd be used to this sort of thing."

"I'm a pilot, not an astronaut."

It was a couple of minutes before Glitch spoke again. "If that's Earth, where are we? The moon?"

Anderson looked at Glitch and raised her eyebrows. "Does this look like the moon?"

Glitch had to concede she had a point. They were standing on the edge of a cave cut high into a wall of red rock that continued far above them. Several hundred feet below lay an apparently endless plain, also red. Dotted across its surface were dozens of scraggy trees, their sickly, pale limbs twisted and bent. A narrow slope led away from the cave and zigzagged down the cliff to the plain below. The sun, their sun, was high in the cloudless sky, and Glitch felt its heat on his skin.

"There's something out there," said Anderson, pointing away to the right.

It took a few seconds for Glitch to see it, but there was a flash of white as the sun caught something metallic, a cluster of structures off in the distance. Glitch peered at it for a minute. "It looks like the Invisitude's city."

"You could be right. Either way, that's where we should be heading."

Glitch wasn't happy with that idea. "You want to go back there? They tried to kill us."

"They also have the only way for us to get home. Unless you've got any better ideas, that's where we need to go."

"But…" Glitch's voice trailed off. Again, he had to concede the point. "How's the doctor?"

Anderson looked down the slope. "She'll be okay, but I'd better go and check on her."

Anderson turned and half walked, half slid back to Doctor Zheng. Glitch took another look at the earth hanging there, so big it felt as though he should be able to touch it, then turned and followed her. The doctor was awake by the time they reached her, and the color was returning to her cheeks. Fido was crouched nearby, eying the glassy slope warily.

As they approached, Doctor Zheng pushed herself up onto her elbows, grimacing at the effort. "What's up there?"

"The earth," said Glitch.

The doctor frowned, and she began struggling to her feet. "What happened? How did we get back to Earth?"

Anderson glared at Glitch. She put a hand on the doctor's shoulder. "You need to stay where you are—take plenty of deep breaths."

"But we have to warn the government."

"We're not on Earth," said Anderson. "I think we're on

a planet in orbit *around* Earth."

Zheng's excitement turned to confusion. "But how is that possible? There are no other habitable planets in our system."

"Well," said Anderson, "there is now."

"It's probably been here all along, but the government has been covering it up," said Glitch.

Anderson looked at him. She seemed unsure whether he was joking, so he gave her his biggest smile. He wasn't a conspiracy theorist. Seeing the mess governments made of running their respective countries, he doubted they could get themselves organized enough to hide an alien needle in a haystack, let alone an entire planet.

"I have to see," said the doctor, her voice filled with a mixture of desperation and excitement.

Anderson held up her hand. "Wait five minutes. At least. Take some deep breaths. You need to get some oxygen into your system. The planet will still be there when you've recovered."

The doctor rolled her eyes and took an exaggeratedly deep breath. Glitch smiled as Anderson shook her head in exasperation.

Slightly less than five minutes later, the three of them were making their way back up the hill, led by the apparently fully recovered Doctor Zheng. They were halfway up the slope when they heard a gruff bark from behind them. Glitch turned to see Fido standing at the foot of the hill, staring pitifully at them.

Glitch stopped. "You go on ahead. I'll catch up." He

began making his way back down the slope.

Fido moaned softly as Glitch got closer. The rock creature stepped forward, his eyes growing wide as his foot skidded on the slick surface. He moaned again.

"Careful, you're starting to sound like a Wookiee. Disney will sue you."

Fido tilted his head.

"Never mind. Look, you don't need to come with us. You can go back."

Glitch stood next to Fido and pointed toward the opening in the wall. Fido looked, but when he turned back, his face was filled with hurt.

"Don't look at me like that. You belong in there. It's safer. You've got family. Probably."

Fido looked up the hill toward Anderson and the doctor. He moaned again. He lifted his foot and slammed it on the ground, trying to force it into the rock. It skidded across the surface, and he growled in frustration.

"You need to go," said Glitch, mustering as much sternness as he could manage as he pointed back toward the crack in the wall.

Fido stamped his foot again, at Glitch this time. Then he took three determined steps up the slope. His feet slipped, and he almost lost his balance. Fido turned back to Glitch and grunted.

"Okay, okay, it's up to you."

Fido turned and started up the slope, Glitch following close behind. By the time they reached the handholds, Fido was crawling on hands and knees. Progress was slow;

every few feet, he slid backward. Fido's groans of frustration were matched only by Glitch's.

Glitch made better progress and reached the holes first. He paused, looking back to watch Fido struggle up the slope.

Fido seemed to relax a little when he saw the holes. He could form his hands into narrow rods and push them into the openings to get some leverage.

Glitch offered a few words of encouragement then reached toward the next hole. As he did, a jet of hot steam burst out of it. More steam sprayed out of another hole to his left and then again from one near his right knee. He heard Fido moan and looked back to see a jet of blisteringly hot water hit Fido in the face. Fido grimaced and shook his head but otherwise seemed unhurt. Glitch scrambled up the slope as quickly as he could, dodging left and right to avoid the increasingly frequent jets of steam.

Glitch heard a muffled roar to his right. Without thinking, he flung himself left, away from the steadily growing noise. Blue fire appeared out of a nearby opening. It seemed almost shy at first, just peeking over the edge, but it quickly spread across the rock until it became a roiling blue carpet. Within seconds, the rock beneath the fire began to blister and burn. Glitch saw it liquefying beneath the strange flames. Heart hammering, he threw himself up the rest of the slope.

As Glitch looked back down the hill, more fire flooded out of the holes. The carpet of flame spread down the slope, steadily gaining speed and rushing toward Fido.

Fido let out a terrified screech.

"Run!" screamed Glitch.

Anderson and the doctor turned and stared in horror at the scene playing out on the slope beneath them.

"Go!" shouted the doctor, waving her arms wildly. "Go!"

Fido let out another cry, his face contorted in terror as the fire rushed toward him.

CHAPTER TWELVE
The Blue Death

Glitch, Anderson, and Zheng discover that the planet they are trapped on appears to be orbiting Earth. They climb out of a cave to investigate, but Fido struggles to cross the cave's glass-like floor. Glitch returns to help him, but as they make their way up the slope, a lethal blue fire erupts from the ground. Glitch manages to get to safety, but Fido is trapped.

Blue fire poured out of the holes, feeding the carpet of flames rolling down the slope, steadily increasing speed. It rushed over the ground toward Fido. He let out a terrified screech.

"Run!" screamed Glitch.

"Go!" shouted the doctor, waving her arms wildly. "Go!"

Fido let out another cry, his face twisted in terror as the fire rushed toward him. He turned and launched himself down the slope. His feet slipped and skidded sideways, sending him crashing onto his face. He slid forward for a moment then got his legs beneath him and pushed, trying to get upright again. He half ran, half fell about twenty feet before the fire caught him.

It wrapped around his ankles, flaring brighter as it found fresh fuel. Fido screamed, tipping his head back in agony. In desperation, he launched himself forward. He crashed into the ground, shards of rock breaking from his body and skittering down the slope. Glitch could see the damage the fire had done in the brief time it had touched Fido. His feet had become two misshapen lumps of charred, blackened rock. Fine wisps of smoke rose steadily from his ankles.

Fido kicked out, desperately trying to find purchase on the slick rock around him. As his right foot hit the ground, it shattered into a dozen pieces. Fido screamed again, a pitiful wailing that tore at Glitch's heart.

Fido rolled onto his back as the fire reached him. The flames flared brighter as they wrapped over his body, engulfing him. Kicking and flailing, he opened his mouth and screamed one last time. The sound cut off as the blue fire rushed into his mouth. He twitched for a few moments, then that too stopped. A few seconds later, as though it realized its work was complete, the blue fire receded. It dispersed slowly, retreating until all that remained was a handful of flickering blue flames hovering above the openings in the rock. Eventually, those too vanished.

Glitch stared down the slope toward the uneven mound of rock where Fido had fallen and cried. He didn't notice Anderson until she placed her hand on his shoulder. He wiped at his face and looked at her.

Her eyes were wet, her jaw clenched tight. "We should go."

Glitch nodded and took one last look down the slope. He'd barely known Fido, didn't even know what sort of creature he was, but he felt his loss as keenly as he had his grandfather's. Whether it was the creature's childlike innocence and playfulness or Glitch's gratitude or just guilt over cultivating a relationship that ultimately led to Fido's death, he wasn't sure. Whatever it was, it made him painfully aware that this wasn't a video game. People could die here. Probably would. Wearily, he turned away and walked with Anderson to the ledge.

Doctor Zheng was waiting for them, and she put her hand on Glitch's shoulder. She seemed uncomfortable with the gesture and opened her mouth to say something, then thought better of it. Glitch nodded, and she removed her hand.

"Do you know where we are? What planet this is?" said Glitch.

The doctor shook her head. "If I wasn't seeing this with my own eyes, I wouldn't believe it. If that's Earth, and there's no evidence to suggest it isn't, we're orbiting at a similar distance to the moon—but on a planet that's approximately four times the size of that moon. Quite apart from the obvious question of why no one has ever seen this planet before, an object this size, this close to Earth would have a dramatic impact on the tides and weather. It's quite impossible to believe that we would not have noticed its existence."

"Unless it's only just arrived," said Anderson.

"I considered that. We have only been here a day, at most, which would imply it somehow moved into orbit within that time frame. That doesn't seem likely either."

"What if it was teleported in?" said Glitch. "Through one of the gateways the Invisitude use."

The doctor raised an eyebrow. "This isn't some ridiculous television show. It would require immense amounts of energy to move a planet, even a relatively small one like this."

"Energy like the Invisitude have? They're literally holding this planet together," said Anderson.

"Barely. I don't think they have the ability to generate that much power."

"So what's your theory?" said Glitch with an edge of frustration in his voice.

"I don't have one," said the doctor simply. "Or at least, not one that makes any more sense than your planet-sized teleportation device."

"Whether we have an explanation or not," said Captain Anderson, "it's pretty clear that the Invisitude are a threat to Earth." The doctor opened her mouth to protest, but Anderson raised her hand. "At least some of them are. We don't know how many people agree with Kurtz, and we don't know what they're capable of. Their technology is far more advanced technology than ours, and we should assume that includes more powerful weapons. We need to get back to Earth."

Glitch looked across the plain toward the Invisitude city. It looked four or five hours away on foot. The ground seemed pretty flat, although the dusty landscape looked far from hospitable. But it did look walkable.

"You're right," said the doctor, standing. "We should go."

Without saying another word, the doctor walked past Glitch and headed down the slope toward the plain. Glitch looked at Anderson and raised his eyebrows.

"Come on," she said.

The path was steep and peppered with rocks, but its uniform width and angle suggested it was artificial. It took them half an hour to reach the bottom of the slope, and the descent was steep enough that they were tired by the time they got to the plain.

They stood for a while, recovering their breath and taking in the view. They were at the base of a huge cliff that stretched as far as they could see in either direction and rose hundreds of feet above them. The plain lay ahead, a broad expanse of flat, red dirt dotted with scrubby trees.

Glitch walked up to one of the trees, a sickly-looking thing about six feet high. It reminded him of a cross between a scrawny, leafless tree and a cactus. Its slender trunk was twisted and bent, leaning so far to the right that it looked ready to collapse. Four withered branches grew from the left-hand side of the trunk, and hanging along their length was a series of green ovoid sacks. Each one was covered with a dozen or so porcupine-like spines and was spattered with a series of charcoal-gray smudges. Glitch tried not to think about how much being speared by one of the spines would hurt.

Doctor Zheng stood by another tree, peering at one of the green cactus-like sacks. "That must be a water store to get them through the dry spells."

"Sort of a horticultural camel," said Glitch.

Glitch was gratified to see the doctor smile. It was slight, but it was definitely a smile.

"Yes, that would be an appropriate description," she said.

Careful to avoid the lethal-looking spines, Glitch pressed a fingertip against one of the green sacks. The skin was soft. It reminded him of the play putty he'd had as a kid and as a student. He pulled his finger away, leaving a gradually fading fingerprint on the surface. A few seconds later, three new spines broke through the surface of the sack where Glitch's finger had been. They grew steadily until they were about three inches long. A pale yellow liquid seeped from the tip of each spine.

"That's incredible," said the doctor. "That's a very rapid defense system."

"I would suggest we all keep clear of the trees and any other plants or animals we see," said Anderson.

"Hmmm," said the doctor absentmindedly. She was peering at the tip of one of the spines. If she got much closer, she'd impale her own eyeball.

"Doctor…" said Anderson.

"Yes, yes." The doctor backed away and, suddenly disinterested in the trees, looked across the plain, searching for the city. When she'd located it, she looked at Captain Anderson. "Shall we carry on, then?"

Anderson nodded, and the doctor turned on her heels and began striding across the plain toward the city. They walked in almost complete silence, the only sound Doctor Zheng's excited oohs and ahhs when they came across an unusual rock or a scraggy piece of plant life they hadn't seen before. More interested in not getting eaten by some sort of alien creature, Glitch kept a wary eye on the desert, searching for signs of life. Every few minutes, the ground rumbled as another earthquake struck. They were less violent here than in the caves but no less disturbing.

Above them, the sky was clear. The relentless sun made sweat run down their backs in uncomfortable rivulets, but Glitch saw a dark patch of cloud forming in the distance, near the horizon.

He was about to point it out to Anderson when something else caught his eye—a flash of silver off to their right. "Captain, there's something over there."

The doctor immediately veered toward the object, once again leading them off across the dusty plain. The trees were thicker here, slowing their progress as they picked their way between them. Even Doctor Zheng was careful to steer well clear of the green sacks. As they walked, Glitch kept an eye on the dark clouds to their right. Whatever it was, it was coming in quickly, the dark-gray mass spreading across the horizon.

The silver object was a rectangular metal box the size of a large truck. Its surface was pitted and scarred. The metal had rotted away completely in places, leaving ragged holes. The front of the box was buckled and half embedded in the dusty ground. Four short cones protruded from its back, a deep gouge stretching out behind it like a tail. A metal cylinder hung from the roof, half torn from its moorings.

"It looks like some sort of vehicle," said Glitch. "It must have crashed here."

Anderson pointed toward the cones. "An aircraft, maybe? Looks like that's the engine."

She tapped her fist against the metal. There was a hollow echoing sound. A door in the side of the aircraft was cracked open enough to create a narrow vertical gap a few inches wide. Glitch went to the opening and peered inside, but it was too dark to see anything. He grabbed the edge of the door.

"Be careful," said Anderson.

Glitch pulled. The door slid backward with a tortured screech. A piece of metal clattered to the ground from somewhere inside, and Glitch jumped. The opening let just enough light into the interior to make out the inside.

Most of the craft was devoted to an open area that contained three empty cages. They were large, big enough to hold four or five people with room to move. Two of them were intact, but the bars of the third were bent outward. Cloth webbing hung from the wall behind the cages, the fabric blackened and rotting. As far as Glitch could tell, the rest of the space was empty.

Glitch turned away from the vehicle, looking back over the plain. "Captain, Doctor—that doesn't look good."

What had started as a strip of dark clouds somewhere near the horizon had quickly grown into a roiling mass of ominous blackness that filled half the sky and blocked out the sun. Dark curtains hung beneath the clouds, and here and there, lightning flickered across its surface. The storm was moving toward them so quickly, they could see its progress. Within a few minutes, it would reach them.

"That's one hell of a storm," said Anderson.

Jagged lightning split the sky in half, and the world flashed blue-white. A few seconds later, thunder reverberated around them, making the ground shake. The hairs on Glitch's neck stood up, the air filled with electricity.

"We should get under cover," said Anderson.

Doctor Zheng pointed across the landscape. "My God, look at the trees."

The rain was clearly visible, a wall of dark gray rushing toward them. And where the rain hit the trees, thick streams of smoke rose into the air.

"Get inside," shouted Anderson. "Quickly."

The world flashed white again, and another wave of thunder pounded their senses. Half blinded by the glare of the lightning, Glitch ducked into the crashed aircraft. He helped the captain inside, but Zheng seemed entranced by the approaching rain.

"Doctor," shouted Anderson.

Doctor Zheng frowned and ignored Anderson for a few seconds. Then she snapped back to reality and sprinted to the opening. Anderson and Glitch helped her inside just as the wall of rain reached them. It pounded against the aircraft, chattering like hail on a tin roof. Lightning flashed again, and with an ear-splitting crack, a nearby tree exploded. Glitch tried desperately to remember the attributes of a Faraday cage in the hope they might be sheltering in one.

The rain grew louder. A thick smell, like burning rubber or plastic, filled the air. Glitch brushed his hand against a fine thread, like spider's silk, hanging from the ceiling. He cursed and rubbed at his hand, hissing. A red line appeared across its back where the thread had grazed him. A few seconds later, a tiny hole opened in the middle of the roof. Another thread dropped into the vehicle. Glitch stepped back as more holes opened, and a cluster of the acidic silk dropped to the floor next to him, hissing and spitting as it hit the metal.

CHAPTER THIRTEEN
Acid Onslaught

Unable to escape the onslaught of the deadly blue fire, Fido is killed. Glitch, Captain Anderson, and Doctor Zheng leave the cave system and begin crossing a vast desert toward a cluster of structures they believe is the Invisitude city. On the way, they discover an aircraft, but their investigation is cut short when a deadly storm arrives.

The rain hammered the roof, and the air was filled with the smell of burning rubber or plastic. Glitch flinched, cursing, when he brushed his hand against a fine thread hanging from the ceiling. He rubbed at a red line that appeared across the back of his hand. A tiny hole opened up in the middle of the ceiling, and another thread dropped through it. As soon as the thread hit the floor of the vehicle, the metal hissed and spat. Glitch dodged backward as another hole opened and a cluster of threads dropped into the aircraft.

"Look out, Captain," said Glitch as a hole opened up

just above Captain Anderson.

She dived to her right, the threads just missing her. Something touched Glitch's ear, and a burning sensation ran down the side of his face. Without thinking, he slapped at his ear, brushing his hand against the thread and burning his fingers, too.

"Move to the back," shouted Anderson.

Glitch wasn't sure how that would help, but he did it anyway. He pushed himself against the metal wall, trying to make himself as small as possible. Someone pressed against him—Anderson, maybe. It was impossible to tell in the gloom. The burning smell was getting stronger, the bitter tang catching in his throat. More and more holes opened in the roof, letting in more of the deadly threads.

Outside, lightning flashed again. Glitch counted off the seconds. One... two... three... four. Thunder shook the aircraft, dislodging more of the silk. The storm was receding. It certainly seemed as though the rain was easing up, but it was hard to tell whether that was reality or Glitch's overactive—and overoptimistic—imagination. If they could hang on, they might make it through this after all.

The three of them sat there, crammed as far back into the aircraft as they could manage, willing the rain to pass. Holes were still opening up in the roof here and there, but they were smaller and there were fewer of them. Gradually the rain—the acid or whatever it was—slowed then stopped. The doctor started to move forward, but Anderson stopped her and pointed.

With the storm clouds moving away, the sky was growing light again, and Glitch saw how lucky they'd been. A dozen or so threads hung from the ceiling. They were thick and silver, and they glistened like Christmas tree ornaments in the light filtering into the aircraft.

Anderson tucked her hand inside the arm of her Air Force jacket. Tentatively, she touched one of the threads. Glitch expected it to burn through her sleeve, but instead, it shattered, drifting slowly to the floor in a cloud of shimmering dust. Anderson tried another of the threads with the same result. She made light work of the rest. They appeared to be harmless now, inert, but she wasn't taking any chances. She worked through the cabin, methodically knocking each of the threads to the floor. Once the room was clear, they made their way back outside.

The storm was still visible far in the distance, the occasional flash of lightning illuminating the black clouds. The impact of the storm was visible everywhere they looked. Every tree was covered in fresh black scars. Many of the green sacks had split, the corrosive threads burning through the soft green skin until they split open or fell to the ground. Damp patches surrounded the fallen pods, confirming the doctor's hypothesis that they were storage sacs for water or some other liquid. Gossamer threads lay all over the ground. There were so many they couldn't help stepping on them, but they'd lost their potency. The doctor even braved touching one hanging from a branch and suffered no ill effects.

Glitch rubbed his ear; it still stung. A red line ran across the fingertips of his right hand where he'd tried to wipe the thread away, and no doubt there was a similar mark on his ear. "This place needs some dragonriders."

"So you can read as well as watch movies," said Anderson. "I'm impressed."

"Audiobook," said Glitch.

Anderson laughed, earning a scowl from the doctor.

"Now I get why the Invisitude live under a dome," said Glitch. "I can't imagine anything surviving those sorts of storms."

"On the contrary," said the doctor. "Even on Earth, many creatures have evolved to survive conditions that humans would find lethal. There are almost certainly creatures that have evolved skins resistant to the threads. Or that can sense the oncoming storm and take shelter, perhaps by burrowing. Even the scenarios created by Anne McCaffrey are not out of the question. Perhaps we have actually traveled to Pern."

"So you've read her books," said Glitch, surprised that the doctor would admit to spending any of her time on something as mundane as popular fiction.

"What can I say? I was a student," said Doctor Zheng, her poker face leaving Glitch unsure as to how to react.

Anderson grinned at the uncertainty on Glitch's face. "Come on, let's get to the city before there's another one of those storms."

As Anderson and Zheng picked their way through the trees, Glitch took one last look at the metal shell that had saved them from the storm. He whispered a quiet thanks to whoever had left it there after the crash.

They'd walked in silence for almost twenty minutes, each of them deep in their own thoughts, when Glitch heard the snap of wood breaking. The noise came from somewhere off to his right. He looked at Anderson. She nodded and pressed a finger to her lips. As they walked, she moved slowly around him until she was walking on his right. Trying to look casual, as though he was simply admiring the view, Glitch looked around. The trees were thick, but he thought he saw a shadow dodging between them.

There was another sound, a low-pitched growl, and this time, the doctor noticed it. "Captain… I don't think we're alone."

"Yeah, they've been following us for the last few minutes."

Ahead of them, a pair of shadows, each about the size of a large dog, flitted between the trees. There was a short, gruff bark from behind them, followed by a second and third from the left and right. Anderson slowed and picked up three branches from the ground, giving one each to Glitch and Zheng. Glitch swung his from side to side. It was light, insubstantial. Whatever those things were, he hoped they were friendly.

The first creature came bounding toward them. It looked like a large dog or a coyote, but instead of fur, it was covered with layer upon layer of thin spines. Its coat was mottled black and beige and rippled as it ran toward them, a deep growl coming from its throat. When the creature got close, Anderson swung her branch. It caught the creature squarely on the side of the head, and it veered to the right, turning away from them before stopping.

A second creature appeared, and a third. They ran toward Glitch, Anderson, and Zheng, weaving through the trees. Their pounding feet kicked up clouds of dust that hung in the air behind them. As they drew near the humans, they slowed, circling them, low growls coming from deep within their throats.

A fourth creature appeared, bigger than the first three. There was a long strip down its right flank where the spines had been ripped away. The flesh beneath was puckered and red. A thick scar ran down its face. The creature stalked toward them, its body close to the ground, muscles rippling beneath the spines. Its eyes—one black, the other a milky white—were filled with menace. A strand of thick red drool dripped from the creature's mouth.

The creature nearest Glitch lunged toward him, and he swung his branch at it. It ducked under the blow but pulled up and backed off anyway. One of the smaller creatures did the same, faking an attack on Doctor Zheng. The animals were probing their defenses, looking for a way through. It wouldn't be long before the creatures realized the branches were useless.

Somewhere in the distance, something howled. There was a brief flicker of darkness as a shadow passed over the group. Glitch looked into the cloudless sky. At first he couldn't see anything, then he spotted four winged creatures circling above.

They were big, larger than any human or the dog creatures. As Glitch watched, one of them spiraled out of the sky and swooped toward the bigger of the four dog-things. The flying creature swept between the trees, a blur of flapping wings. It hit the dog, knocking it sideways, before climbing back into the sky.

"Run," yelled Anderson, waving toward the city.

Glitch didn't need any more encouragement. Dodging between the trees, he ran as hard as he could, the doctor close behind. Another shadow passed over him. Not daring to look up, he dodged left, ducking under a branch and into a thicker clump of trees. There was a rush of air across his neck.

Glitch glanced to the right. The doctor was running parallel to him, ducking and diving through the trees. He saw no sign of Captain Anderson, the dog-things, or the birds. Ahead, the trees thinned out, giving way to a wide-open plain that gradually sloped upward. The city was visible in the distance, but there was no way he'd make it before the creatures caught him.

"Stay in the trees," he shouted.

He turned right, toward the doctor. She hadn't heard him. She crashed through the edge of the trees and out into the open plain. She hesitated, and for a moment, Glitch thought she'd turn back. Then she dipped her head and sprinted off. Cursing, Glitch looked back. Anderson was a few feet behind him, still weaving through the trees.

"It's too exposed," shouted Glitch.

"Doctor!" shouted Anderson.

This time Zheng heard. She slid to a halt and spun around. Anderson shouted to her to get back under cover, and Zheng immediately started running back. Two black shapes swooped overhead. The creatures looked like giant eagles, their legs thin and featherless but muscular.

Doctor Zheng screamed when the first creature hit her, knocking her backward onto the ground. Glitch ran toward her. The ground was soft, sandy, and dotted with holes, making progress difficult. By the time Glitch got to the doctor, the creature was crouched on top of her. As he approached, it turned toward him.

For the most part, the creature's face was humanoid, but it was flatter, as though its head had been pressed against a sheet of glass while the skull was still soft. Its eyes were bigger, too, round and dark, and instead of a nose and mouth, it had a beak. The creature's body was a curious mix of human and bird. Its two legs ended in elongated feet with four toes that curled over into lethal-looking talons. It had arms as well as wings covered in brown and gray feathers. Its body was sleek and smooth, muscular and dangerous looking. The creature looked male, although, despite its nudity, there was no way to tell.

The doctor bucked and twisted but couldn't work herself free from beneath the creature. Anderson appeared at Glitch's side and advanced toward the bird thing. Another one landed in front of Anderson, blocking her progress. Its great wide wings stirred up plumes of dust as it touched down. It stood upright, like a man, watching Anderson and Glitch.

After a minute or two, the new arrival let out a sharp trill. Immediately, the creature crouched on the doctor flapped its wings, and lifted off. It flew backward a few feet then landed again.

Now that they were side by side, Glitch saw that the second creature was several inches taller than the first, and its muscles were more defined. Two more of the creatures landed nearby in a rustle of feathers and dust.

The doctor rolled to her feet and quickly backed away until she was standing beside Anderson. She lifted her arm, twisting her shoulder to check for damage. Despite her ordeal, her face was full of wonder. "I've never seen anything like them."

The taller creature stepped forward, and Anderson tensed. Whatever it was, it seemed to be the leader of the group. The others were hanging back, waiting for it to make its move.

"My name is Zheng," said the doctor, tapping her chest.

The creature tipped its head to one side and blinked.

Zheng stepped forward, her arms open. "Please, we wish you no harm."

Glitch had to stifle a laugh. It seemed unlikely they were the ones capable of doing the harming. Zheng glared at him and took another step forward. As she did, the ground in front of her gave way. Zheng screamed as she slid toward the hole, desperately clawing at the sand.

Anderson dived forward, reaching for Zheng. Their fingertips touched for a second, then Zheng vanished into the still-growing sinkhole. The captain managed to get back to her feet, but as she ran toward Glitch, another sinkhole opened. Within seconds, they were both sliding down a steep, sand-covered slope.

CHAPTER FOURTEEN
Sandfall

As Glitch, Captain Anderson, and Doctor Zheng shelter inside a crashed aircraft, deadly acidic threads rain down upon them, burning through the shell of the vehicle. The storm passes, and they are able to continue their journey across the desert toward the Invisitude city. But soon they are pursued by four dog-like, spine-covered animals. A group of winged creatures attack the dogs but quickly turn on the humans. Cornered, Doctor Zheng attempts to communicate with them.

Doctor Zheng stepped toward the leader of the winged creatures. As she did, the ground in front of her gave way. The sandy ground collapsed, vanishing into a sinkhole. Zheng slid, screaming, toward the opening. Anderson dived forward, clutching at Zheng's hand. Their fingertips touched for a second, then Zheng vanished out of sight.

Anderson pushed herself back to her feet and ran toward Glitch. A second sinkhole opened, and within seconds, Glitch and Anderson were both plummeting down a steep, sand-covered slope.

Sand sprayed into Glitch's face, blinding him and filling his mouth before he could close it. Spitting out the sand, he kicked, trying to slow his descent. His right foot caught something hard, sending a jarring pain up his leg. He yelled as he was flipped sideways, his arm twisting awkwardly beneath him. His mouth filled with sand again. Then the ground beneath him vanished and he was falling through the air, sand streaming around him like a waterfall.

He landed with a dull thud on a high drift of sand. The impact knocked the wind out of him. Rolling onto his side, he spat out the latest mouthful of sand. There was another thump as Captain Anderson hit the ground a few feet away, her head just inches from a sharp chunk of rock that lay half buried in the sand.

Glitch got to his knees as sand rained down around him. He stumbled across the constantly shifting sands toward Anderson, his mind filled with visions of being buried alive. She was standing too, a few feet from where she'd landed and away from the torrent of sand streaming down.

"Where's Doctor Zheng?"

Glitch shook his head.

"I'm here." Zheng was standing to their right, underneath a curved piece of rock that jutted from the wall and was barely visible in what little light filtered in from the hole above.

They picked their way across the sand pile toward her.

"Are you okay?" asked Zheng.

They nodded. As his eyes adjusted to the gloom, Glitch looked around. They'd fallen through a tall vertical tube, like a well, and landed on a mound of sand inside a bowl-shaped cave. It was gloomy, and the edges of the cave were hidden in shadow, but the walls looked smooth, glassy. Glitch thought of the blue flames that had consumed Fido and wondered if they'd just fallen out of the proverbial frying pan.

The sand falling into the cave slowed to a trickle. Wherever they were, at least there was no danger of any premature burials. There was no sign of the bird creatures, either. But as the final remnants of sand drifted to the ground, Glitch heard a noise—something scraping against rock. A shadow darted across the edge of his vision. He felt Anderson tense, but Zheng took a couple of steps forward.

"Please, we're not here to hurt you," the doctor said.

Glitch stifled a groan as another shadow moved around the edge of the cave. Zheng held out her hands and moved forward again.

"Doctor Zheng," hissed Anderson.

"It's okay, Captain." Zheng walked slowly down the mound and onto the floor of the cave, Anderson and Glitch close behind. When she reached ground level, she stopped. "Please. Show yourself."

With a quiet shuffling sound, a figure walked out of the gloom. A soft light flared. The creature was holding a globe similar to the ones Glitch and Anderson had seen in the caves, but this one was white.

The light it gave off was strong, and it was enough to give them a better look at the creature. It was naked, its skin a pasty white. Its head was hairless with two large eyes, black orbs bulging from the pale skin. Its mouth was just a small horizontal slit, and it didn't seem to have a nose. Glitch's overall impression was that it was some sort of bipedal mole. Glitch wondered if it would consider that an insult. Here and there, clumps of red mud clung to the wrinkles and folds in its flesh as though it had been playing in the dirt.

"Welcome," said the creature in a deep baritone. "My name is Lith."

Glitch frowned. He heard the words, but they weren't being spoken aloud. Instead, they were simply appearing in his mind, springing fully formed from nothing. Lith's speech was a little stilted. Each word came slowly, deliberately, like someone learning a new language.

Glitch looked at Anderson. "Do you hear that?"

Anderson nodded.

The doctor stepped forward, eyes wide. "You speak... English?"

"In a way, yes. We are able to communicate... directly with you in a way your mind is able to interpret."

"Like telepathy?" said Anderson.

Lith's forehead creased. "I am sorry, I do not understand."

"Can you read our minds? See what we're thinking?"

Lith shook his head. "Ah, I understand. No, we cannot

perceive your thoughts and feelings. We can only interpret the words you speak in a limited way."

Anderson looked uncertain, but Glitch thought the doctor might explode. She walked toward Lith, her hand outstretched. Lith eyed it cautiously then tentatively reached out. His hand was long and oval. He had no fingers as such, just a single break splitting the paddle-like hand in two.

Zheng grabbed Lith's hand and pumped it enthusiastically. "It's such an honor to meet you, Lith. My name is Doctor Zheng, that is Captain Anderson on the right, and Dwayne Mitchell on the left."

"Thank you, Doctor Zheng. I hope none of you are pained."

Glitch lifted his right leg, frowning as his ankle complained about the movement, but Zheng waved her hand. "No, no, not at all."

"Good. I am relieved. Perhaps you are hungry?"

"Yes," said Glitch, before the doctor could speak on his behalf. "We haven't had much to eat since we got here."

"If you are pleased to follow me, I can provide you with food and water."

Anderson opened her mouth to reply, but before she could say anything, the doctor flung out her arms. "That would be very kind, thank you."

Anderson closed her mouth, her lips pressed tight.

Lith led them through an intricate series of tunnels, branching left and right, climbing and falling. Glitch lost his sense of direction within minutes, and he had no idea whether they were moving nearer or farther away from the city. As they walked, Glitch argued with his stomach about the relative merits of eating versus trying to get back home to warn Earth. In the end, his stomach won. After all, it wouldn't do Earth any good if they passed out from lack of food before they got there.

Eventually they rounded a corner and found themselves looking at a huge open cavern. The far side of the cave was shrouded in darkness, the ceiling barely visible. Dozens of glowing poles provided light at ground level. To Glitch, they looked like giant glow sticks that emitted the soft white of Lith's orb rather than a nuclear green. Dotted around the cave were row upon row of huts and long mounds that looked uncomfortably like giant graves—a shanty town built of mud and sticks. Glitch did a quick count and reached the conclusion that there were at least forty homes, and those were just the ones that were visible. There could easily be a lot more in the shadows.

The village was populated by dozens of creatures like Lith. Groups of them walked around or sat outside the huts and tents. They talked to each other in quick, breathless hisses and gasps, adding a static-like background noise to the scene. Children, smaller versions of Lith, sat on the ground playing with woven toys or chased each other through the legs of the adults.

As Glitch and the others approached the center of the village, the conversations died away. A few of the braver children followed them, peering at the new arrivals, unabashedly curious. Soon they had a procession of children following them through the village. The ground beneath their feet shook as another earthquake struck. No one seemed to take much notice, but Glitch eyed the ceiling, alert to falling debris.

They reached a long building, four or five times the size of the largest one they'd passed up to that point. A group of adults was gathered outside. They were standing around an animal being roasted above a mound of glowing red rocks. Glitch felt the heat from several feet away, but he didn't recognize the animal until they got close. It was one of the dog-like creatures that had attacked them above ground—a particularly large specimen, even with its spines removed. Without thinking, Glitch peered at its head to see if it had a scar. It didn't.

Lith gestured for them to sit. "My people welcome you."

Glitch couldn't quite get used to the pseudo-telepathy. It felt as if his mind was itchy.

"May I ask," said Zheng, "what do your people call yourselves?"

Lith hesitated, looking around the village. "You have no words for us, but you can call us the So-lang. That is similar."

"So-lang…" said Zheng. "Thank you."

Glitch leaned close to Anderson. "Better than mole-men."

Zheng elbowed him in the ribs, her eyes blazing. Glitch winced and felt his face flush.

Two of the So-lang arrived carrying a long wooden

pole, clearly the trunk of a tree significantly healthier than the ones they'd seen in the desert. Suspended on the pole was a leather basket filled with more rocks. The pole carriers' bodies were covered in sweat, either from the heat or from the exertion, and Glitch imagined he could smell singed skin. They lowered the bucket to the ground near the roasting creature and removed the pole. Then they lifted the bucket and added the rocks to the mound. Fat dripped from the roasting meat and sizzled on the rocks beneath. Glitch's stomach rumbled.

Lith smiled and motioned toward a young boy who was standing nearby, holding a rough stone knife. Lith made a couple of quick sounds, like gasps, and the boy responded in kind. Then he grabbed a flat piece of wood from a pile next to him, hacked a few slices of meat off the creature onto the wood, and passed it to Glitch.

The pink meat smelled delicious, but Glitch waited until Lith and Anderson had their own servings. His mother had taught him nothing if not how to be polite at mealtimes. When the boy offered a plate to the doctor, she declined. Lith stared at her for a moment, as though he might be offended, then shrugged, grabbed a handful of meat, pushed it into his mouth, and chewed noisily. He smiled and nodded toward the boy, a trickle of grease running down his chin. He gestured to Glitch to eat.

Glitch gave Zheng a questioning look.

Zheng gave him a tight smile. "I'm a vegetarian."

Glitch considered making a comment about alien meat being murder then changed his mind and just nodded. A young girl hesitantly brought them each a wooden cup filled with water. Glitch smiled and thanked her. He sipped the water. It was crisp and cool, refreshing.

Glitch looked at the meat for a moment, summoning up the courage to try it. Anderson seemed to be enjoying her food, although less conspicuously than Lith, so he picked out the smallest scrap of meat he could find and tentatively dropped it into his mouth. He'd been expecting chicken, but it was actually closer to ham, although with a rougher texture. It was juicy and a little sweet, and he had to agree it was good. His stomach growled again, urging him to hurry up. Anderson smiled, and he blushed as he grabbed another chunk of meat.

Every time their plates got anywhere close to being empty, the young boy rushed over with another pile of food. Finally Glitch and Anderson had to wave him away, rubbing their bellies in the universal sign of "No more for me, I've eaten too much already."

Anderson groaned.

"Do you think they have any wafer-thin mints?" said Glitch in an exaggerated French accent.

Anderson grimaced, and for a second, Glitch thought he'd put his foot in it again. Then she smiled and shook her head in mock despair.

A crowd of the So-lang had gathered around the roasting animal, most of them with their own plates or holding great chunks of meat in their hands. A few of the children gathered nearby, surreptitiously watching the visitors as they tucked into their own food. It seemed such a normal scene, like something Glitch might read about in *National Geographic* while he waited for a haircut. He could almost forget they were on an impossible planet orbiting Earth. Only the alien features of the people around him made it seem anything other than normal.

Lith let out a long, enthusiastic belch. The children laughed with delight and promptly began trying to outdo him, and each other, with longer and louder burps. Glitch was tempted to join in but couldn't quite muster the courage. Then Anderson let out a surprisingly rip-roaring belch, and Glitch found himself digging deep and adding his own accompaniment. Even Doctor Zheng managed to add her own meager burp to the mix.

The belching contest was just beginning to die away when the first bird-man burst through the cavern ceiling. Lumps of rock crashed to the floor, destroying one of the smaller huts and sending people running. Screams filled the air as three more of the winged creatures appeared. They were carrying iron bars with long leather strips attached to the ends, and as they swept over the village, they swung the whips at the fleeing So-lang.

Lith pointed at the bird-men. "Barash!"

The village erupted into chaos. The So-lang scattered, some running into buildings, others trying to get to the safety of the tunnels. A few stood still, too terrified to move.

Glitch watched in horror as one of the Barash caught a young So-lang, flicking the leather whip around his neck and lifting him into the air. The boy screamed, scrabbling at the leather and trying to free himself as he was dragged upward and out of sight.

More and more Barash appeared until there were too many for Glitch to count. He recognized one of the creatures as the leader they'd met on the surface. It hovered in midair, clicking and shrieking, giving orders to the others. When it saw Glitch, it pointed and emitted three sharp clicks, clearly audible above the shouts and screams of the So-lang panicking. A pair of Barash turned and swooped toward Glitch.

Anderson was crouched next to the doctor, a few feet away. "Get down!"

Glitch dived to the ground as the first of the Barash reached him. He felt the sting of leather on his right calf and yelled.

"We have to get inside," said Anderson, pointing toward the large building.

The door was open, and several of the So-lang were trying to get to it past the circling Barash.

"We won't make it," said Glitch.

Two children, young girls, were cowering behind a wooden table that had been flipped onto its side. One of the Barash landed and strode toward them, flicking its whip ominously. The doctor picked up a nearby rock and threw it at the advancing bird-man. It bounced off its shoulder, but the creature ignored it and continued toward the girls.

Something hit one of the huts near Glitch. A few seconds later, flames flickered to life. Thick black smoke filled the air, drifting over the village and cutting visibility.

Glitch ran toward the burning hut and pulled at a branch sticking out from its base. There was a loud *crump* as something inside the hut exploded. Glitch shouted in frustration as flames engulfed the hut. He tugged harder on the burning branch, and it finally broke free.

Glitch ran toward the children and put himself between the girls and the approaching bird-man, hoping it was afraid of fire. It wasn't. The Barash advanced toward Glitch, the fire from the branch flickering in its eyes. Glitch jabbed the branch at the Barash then swung it at its head. The tip caught the Barash in the eye, and it let out a long, high-pitched screech.

Glitch turned to the girls. "Run!" He waved, urging them to get away, but they stayed crouched behind the table, eyeing the burning building with growing concern.

Doctor Zheng ran toward them. One of the Barash saw her and whirled, swooping after her. Zheng saw the whip flashing toward her a fraction of a second too late. The thin strip of leather wrapped around her arm, and she was pulled backward and up. She screamed in pain and clutched at the whip, trying to support her weight and stop herself from falling.

Three of the Barash landed near Anderson, surrounding her. One of them made a rapid clicking sound and tilted its head.

"I don't know what you're saying," said Anderson, "but I'm guessing you're not asking me on a date."

She ran, dodging left between two of the Barash. They lunged at her, grabbing her shoulder. Anderson twisted, pulled herself loose, and ran toward a nearby cluster of huts.

With a crack, a whip wrapped around Anderson's ankle. She took another step before her leg was yanked backward, sending her crashing to the ground. Her face hit the dirt, splitting her lip. The Barash pulled on its whip, dragging Anderson across the ground. She grabbed at the earth around her, trying to find purchase but failing. The Barash grabbed her beneath her shoulders and lifted into the air.

"No!" screamed Glitch, and he threw the burning branch at the advancing Barash.

The creature batted it away and kept coming. Glitch backed away to find a way out. He glanced left, past the large building, and spotted a narrow tunnel far too small for the Barash to get through but maybe large enough for him. He turned and ran.

As he darted between a couple of huts, a shadow reared up out of the smoke. The leader of the Barash swept toward him, wings outstretched as it glided across the cavern. It hit Glitch, knocking him backward and sending him crashing to the ground. The Barash landed on top of Glitch, grabbed him by the shoulders, and slammed him into the floor. Glitch's head snapped backward, cracking against the hard-packed earth.

Glitch struggled to push the Barash off, but the creature was too strong. It smashed Glitch's head into the ground again. Glitch's vision swam. The Barash stopped hitting Glitch's head against the ground, and Glitch felt himself being lifted.

CHAPTER FIFTEEN
Prisoners in Peril

After falling through a sinkhole, Glitch, Captain Anderson, and Doctor Zheng find themselves in the company of a So-lang, a pale mole-like creature that can communicate with them telepathically. The So-lang, Lith, takes the humans back to his village, where they enjoy a meal and a spirited belching competition. As the group begins to relax, a troop of bird-people, the Barash, attack the village. Despite their best efforts, Captain Anderson and Doctor Zheng are caught and carried away as Glitch faces down one of the Barash.

Glitch hurled the burning branch at the Barash, but the creature simply batted it away and kept walking. Glitch backed away, searching for an escape. Glancing to his left, he spotted a narrow tunnel too small for the Barash to get through. He ran toward it.

He was almost halfway there when a shadow reared up in front of him. Glitch looked up to see the leader of the Barash gliding across the village toward him.

The creature knocked Glitch over then landed on top of him. It slammed Glitch's head into the ground. Glitch struggled to push the Barash off, but the creature was too strong, too heavy. The creature cracked Glitch's head against the ground again. Glitch's vision swam, and he felt himself being lifted off the ground.

Glitch twisted and turned in the Barash's grip as the creature carried him higher and higher. Glitch knew what was about to happen. He'd seen crows do this with shellfish on the beach. The Barash would carry him to the ceiling then drop him on the village below. He'd crack open, spilling his delicious brains all over the floor, and the Barash would land and go all *Walking Dead* on him.

He was still waiting for the Barash to let him go when they passed through the hole in the ceiling and back into the open air above the desert. The sudden change in light and perspective set Glitch's stomach rolling and churning. He felt bile rising toward his throat and vomited, half-digested meat falling to the desert below. The Barash leveled off before it curved right, away from the city, and flew parallel to the cliff they'd descended to get to the plain.

Once his stomach was under control again, Glitch twisted around, trying to find the doctor and Anderson. Other Barash passed nearby, flying in formation with people in their arms or hanging from whips beneath them.

Glitch searched the Barash's victims, but none of them appeared to be human. Glitch wasn't sure whether he was happy about that or not. He figured he had a better chance of surviving with Anderson there to help fight off the Barash. If the doctor could put aside her scientific curiosity for long enough, she might be able to help too. Still, he'd rather they were safe, even if that meant he was destined for a grisly end.

Glitch closed his eyes. The bobbing motion of the Barash's flight was making him nauseated, and his stomach was threatening to let loose another stream of vomit. He focused on the air rushing past him and tried not to think about the distance between him and the desert floor or what would happen to him if the Barash lost its grip.

When Glitch opened his eyes again, he could see their destination. Or at least he assumed the cluster of tall trees dotted with huts was a Barash village. Long wooden suspension bridges linked the buildings, and Glitch saw Barash moving along them.

More of the creatures flew between the trees or circled above them. For a moment, Glitch felt some of Doctor Zheng's wonder, but then another of the Barash swept in front of him. The young boy Glitch had seen captured was hanging limply beneath the creature, the leather whip still wrapped around his neck.

The Barash pulled right, turning away from the treetop village and toward a large tree that stood slightly apart from the rest. Glitch's Barash followed. It flapped its wings a few times, speeding up until it was leading the group. The tree housed over a dozen cages. Most of them were empty, but a couple had people in them; huddled forms crouched inside, watching the arrival of the newcomers.

Glitch's Barash swept toward one of the larger cages, near the top of the tree. As they got close, two unladen Barash swooped past. They landed on top of the cage, unhooked a door, and swung it open. The creature carrying Glitch slowed as they approached the cage, then it hovered above it. Glitch realized what was about to happen just as the Barash let him go.

The floor of the cage was covered in a thick layer of leaves and branches, a concession to comfort. But still, it hurt when Glitch landed. And it smelled. The floor covering looked fresh, but apparently en suite bathrooms were not a feature of Barash prisons.

Dusting himself off, Glitch stood and moved to the side of the cage, peering through the wooden bars at the other people being carried to their cells. The Barash carrying the young boy circled the tree as though looking for somewhere to land. To Glitch's horror, it gave the leather whip a shake, and the boy plummeted to the ground, bouncing through the branches before landing with a soft crunch that made Glitch's blood run cold.

Glitch looked around, terrified of what he might see. A dozen or so of the Barash were flying around the tree. Some of them were still carrying their captives; others had already deposited them in their cells and had taken up position as guards or lookouts.

Most of the occupied cages held So-lang. Without exception, they sat on the floor, heads bowed as though they had resigned themselves to their fate. There were a couple of other humanoid forms that Glitch didn't recognize, but they were too big to be either Zheng or Anderson.

There was a noise from somewhere above Glitch, and he turned to see one of the So-lang, a young male by the looks of it, dropped through the door of the cage. The So-lang landed on the floor with a solid thud and lay there, groaning.

The cage door clicked shut. The So-lang groaned again. He was bare chested and had red welts around his waist where the whip had cut into him. Glitch reached to press his fingers against the So-lang's neck then realized he had no idea whether So-lang had pulses or how he might measure one. He pulled his hand away. The So-lang opened his eyes and saw Glitch. His face filled with fear, and he tried to push himself backward.

Glitch tentatively put a hand on the So-lang's shoulder then pulled it away when he flinched.

"It's okay," said Glitch. "You're safe."

The So-lang shook his head forcefully. "Not safe. Not here."

He had a point.

"Okay… maybe not forever, but for now you're safe. You can get some rest while I figure a way out."

"No way out."

"Okay, so you're a glass-half-empty kind of guy. I get it."

The So-lang frowned, puzzled.

"Never mind. Safe or not, you need some rest. My

164

name's Glitch."

"I am Nen."

"Okay, Nen, lie there and get some sleep."

Nen nodded and closed his eyes. Glitch peered at Nen's neck for a moment, looking for a pulse, then realized that might be considered more than a little creepy and stood. The world swam around him as blood rushed to his head. He rested his hand against the cage. The bars were wooden, bound with thin green vines.

When he'd recovered his balance, Glitch tugged on the bars. They barely moved, and they were too thick and solid to break without some sort of weapon. Glitch picked at one of the vines, but the skin was too hard. It was more like wire than vegetation.

Glitch shivered. It was growing dark and getting cold. Looking at his T-shirt, now covered in brown dust and with a rip in the right sleeve, he wondered just how cold the planet got. He wasn't dressed for interplanetary adventures.

Looking out over the village, he saw the Barash gliding between the trees and walking across the wooden bridges—going about their daily lives. It seemed such a normal scene—apart from the flying bird-people and cages full of prisoners. Glitch glanced back at his fellow captive. Nen's eyes were still closed, but Glitch could see his pale chest slowly rising and falling.

Glitch searched the trees for Anderson and Zheng again, and this time he found them. They were lower down the tree in a slightly smaller cage. It seemed to just be the two of them. Anderson was pressed against the bars, trying to get a better view of the village. Glitch could barely make her out in the growing darkness, but presumably she was looking for him. He slipped his hand through the cage and waved to her.

After a couple of minutes of frantic waving, he got her attention, and she waved back. Then Glitch realized just how much like a worm his arm looked. Visions of ravenous bird-people swooping on his pale flesh flashed through his head, and he quickly pulled his arm back into the cage. He wondered whether he should call down to Anderson to let her know he was all right. Then a shadow flickered across his cage as one of the Barash flew overhead, and he decided to keep quiet.

He watched Anderson in her cage. The doctor appeared at her side, and Anderson pointed at Glitch. It took a while for the doctor to spot him, but eventually she gave a little wave.

Glitch watched Anderson explore the cage, testing the bars just as he had. Eventually, she sat on the floor, back pressed against the side of the cage.

It was almost dark, and pinpricks of light were appearing all over the village. Glitch could make out the flickering glow of a fire through the windows of some of the huts and another, much larger fire in the middle of the village, half hidden by the trees and platforms. Shapes moved across the flames, and he imagined the Barash standing around a roast, just as the So-lang had.

Glitch checked on Nen again. He was still asleep, still

breathing. Sighing, Glitch lay on the floor and tried not to think about what might be crawling toward him through the tree.

Glitch was woken shortly after dawn by the clattering of a wooden plate scraping against the bars of the cage. One of the Barash was crouched on top of the cage, a large wooden bowl and another plate sitting next to it.

Glitch sat up, his bones cracking and complaining at the disturbance. Nen stirred, too, and the Barash grabbed a couple of handfuls of leafy vegetables from the bowl and dropped them onto the plates. Then it unlatched the cage door and dropped the plates and a leather pouch into the cage. The plates hit the floor and bounced, scattering the food everywhere. Glitch stared at the mess as the Barash closed the cage door and flew away. It was hard to tell where the food ended and the floor began.

Nen rolled over, groaning, and crawled to the food. He picked at it for a moment, sniffed it, then started eating. Glitch considered ignoring breakfast. He wasn't sure how long he'd slept, but it wasn't long enough for him to get really hungry. But he had no idea how long it would be before their next meal. If this was all he was going to get, he'd better make the most of it.

He joined Nen, grabbed what he hoped was food, and put it on one of the plates. "Good morning."

Nen nodded but didn't speak. It looked as though his earlier terror had receded, but he was clearly still scared.

Glitch bit into a long, thin vegetable. It looked like a white carrot but tasted watery and bitter.

He grabbed the leather pouch and shook it. It sloshed. "Is this water?"

Nen looked up from his food, glanced at the pouch, then shrugged. "Probably."

Glitch pulled the wooden stopper from the pouch and sniffed at it. All he could smell was musty leather. He poured a little of the liquid into his hand. A few particles of what Glitch hoped was just leaf floated on the surface, but otherwise it looked like water.

"Here goes nothing." He lapped at the water in his hand. It seemed normal enough. He poured some of it from the pouch directly into his mouth, trying not to think about what else might be in it. The water had an earthy undertaste, but it was cool and refreshing. Glitch offered the pouch to Nen, but he shook his head.

"No, thank you."

Glitch took another sip then replugged the pouch and placed it on the ground. He picked at the food on his plate. It all tasted much the same—grassy. He was pretty sure the last thing he tried actually was grass. He spat it out.

Once his plate was empty and he couldn't find anything more that looked like food among the vegetation on the floor, Glitch stood. His ankle was tender from his fall down the sinkhole, and he rotated it a few times, trying to loosen it. Once he got bored of that, he went to check on Anderson and the doctor.

The sun was low over the horizon, its warmth chasing away the fine layer of mist that had descended over the village. The dim light made it hard to see, but he thought he could make out Anderson and the doctor sitting in their cage with their own food. Anderson was quietly eating hers, but the doctor was peering at her plate, gesturing excitedly. Apparently she approved of the Barash's vegetarian fare.

With a soft thud, a pair of Barash landed on top of Glitch's cage. They were big and muscular, and their arrival made the cage rock slightly. They both carried the same whips used in the attack on the So-lang village. The Barash flipped the door open and rolled a rope ladder into the cage. One of them let out a series of rapid, rather aggressive chirps.

"He wants us to go with them," said Nen.

Without waiting for a response from Glitch, he walked slump-shouldered over to the rope ladder and climbed up. When he was almost at the top, one of the bird-men grabbed him and hauled him out by the shoulders. Nen flinched but didn't resist or make a sound.

Glitch got similar treatment. Standing on top of the cage with the Barash's claw-like hands wrapped around his wrist, Glitch wondered exactly where they thought he would run. They were at least a hundred feet above ground, with dozens of lethal-looking branches just waiting to crack skulls and break spines.

Below them, Glitch saw Anderson pulled out of her cage. She looked at him and waved. Glitch tried to respond, but the Barash tightened its grip on Glitch's wrist. Glitch's hand was beginning to go numb.

The Barash holding Nen let out a short chirp and pulled on his arm. This time Nen yelled. The Barash unfolded broad wings, black and flecked with red. One was damaged; some of the feathers were missing, and the wingtip was bent at a slight angle. The Barash shook his wings twice then took off, carrying Nen upward a few feet before gliding out over the trees.

As his own captor took off, Glitch tried to steel himself for the inevitable vertigo.

He failed.

As they passed over the edge of the canopy, he made the mistake of looking at the ground far below. His stomach lurched, simultaneously threatening to tie itself into knots and drag itself out of his throat. The breakfast he'd just eaten clawed up his throat, and it was all he could do not to throw up.

They glided down into the forest in a slow circle. Another Barash joined them, its body covered in multicolored streaks and swirls of paint. It paid no attention to Nen but stared at Glitch, apparently intrigued.

When they'd dropped thirty feet or so, the Barash flapped their wings and swept through the village. They picked up speed as they weaved between trees and over walkways. Glitch couldn't help but think that if they ever made a video game of his adventures, this would make one hell of a level.

Glitch heard a squeal. Anderson and the doctor were also being carried through the village, following a parallel path. Anderson looked as though she was actually enjoying the ride. The doctor, less so.

They curved between a pair of trees, narrowly missing a group of young Barash crouched among the branches, then entered a wide, open space. At its center sat a huge tree, its trunk at least thirty feet across. A wide wooden platform circled it, suspended on dozens of thick vines attached to the branches above. At least a dozen Barash stood around the tree, all of them watching Glitch's approach.

The Barash glided low over the platform then let go of Glitch. He landed awkwardly, and his ankle cried out. There was a flutter of wings, and the black-winged Barash landed next to Glitch. A few seconds later, Nen, Anderson, and Doctor Zheng were deposited on the platform beside him.

"Are you okay?" said Anderson.

Glitch nodded, his attention drawn to one of the Barash that had been waiting for them. It stood a few feet away on a wooden dais, but even taking that into account, it was over a foot taller than any of the others, and it was broad and muscular. Like the Barash that had followed Glitch to the platform, its body was covered with a complex series of multicolored patterns—streaks of vibrant reds and greens, circles of ochre and blue. The creature's beak-like mouth was scarlet, as though it had been dipped in blood. Two other Barash stood next to it, smaller and without the markings but no less intimidating.

Glitch shuddered. He leaned down and whispered to Nen, "Who is that?"

"He is the Lorock, their holy leader."

The Lorock walked toward them, back straight, imperious. As he walked, his wings expanded behind him. The feathers shimmered blue and green in the dawn light.

"Hello, my name—" said the doctor.

The Barash behind her let out a screech, and the doctor stopped speaking.

The Lorock walked up to Anderson, looking her up and down. She swallowed, her hands balled into fists. He turned toward the doctor, regarding her with equal indifference, then moved on to Glitch. Glitch looked into his black, soulless eyes, trying to hold the creature's gaze. He couldn't, and Glitch turned away.

The Lorock walked across the platform, making a rapid clicking sound. Nen immediately knelt. A hand grabbed Glitch's shoulder, digging into his flesh and pressing him downward. Glitch let himself be pushed to his knees. The doctor did the same, but Anderson resisted. The Barash behind her kicked at her leg, catching her behind the knee. She grunted and joined them on the floor.

Another Barash appeared, stepping silently from the shadows. It carried a long sword, the blade black with jagged teeth running along both edges. The Barash bowed slightly and placed the sword across its arm, offering the hilt to the Lorock. The Lorock took it with both hands and raised it above his head, letting out a long, deep screech. All around them, the call was repeated, dozens of voices echoing the cry. The Lorock lowered the sword, and the cries stopped as he walked toward Glitch, the vicious-looking blade held out in front of him.

CHAPTER SIXTEEN
Trial in the Treetops

The Barash carry Glitch to their treetop village. He is separated from Captain Anderson and Doctor Zheng and imprisoned with a young male So-lang called Nen. In the morning, Nen and Glitch are woken by the Barash, who feed them a meager breakfast then take all three humans and Nen to a wooden platform in the center of the village. The Lorock, the Barash's spiritual leader, is waiting for them.

The Lorock walked across the platform, making a rapid clicking sound, and a Barash appeared and forced all four of them to their knees.

A second Barash walked out of the shadows, carrying a long black sword, the blade edged with jagged teeth. The Barash gave the blade to the Lorock, who raised it above his head and let out a long, deep screech. The Barash standing around the platform repeated the call until the air was filled with their cries. When the Lorock fell silent, the rest followed his lead.

The Lorock lowered the sword, holding it out in front of his body, and walked toward Glitch.

Glitch looked at Anderson. He saw her tense, preparing to run at the Lorock when he got close enough. He hoped that was before the Barash ran Glitch through or cut his head off or whatever he was planning on doing. The rest of the Barash's excitement was clear, a tangible bloodlust that Glitch could actually feel. The Lorock approached Glitch and lifted the black sword again. Glitch stared at it, praying Anderson would make her move soon.

There was a flurry of activity, and a murmur spread through the Barash as a shape glided from the branches above and landed softly between Glitch and the Lorock. It was the painted Barash who'd followed them into the village. It folded its wings and walked toward the Lorock, arms open as if it was going to give him a hug. Scowling, the Lorock lowered the sword.

As the multicolored Barash approached, the Lorock let out a rapid series of low clicks and whistles. It responded by bowing slightly and making a soft trilling sound. The Lorock looked at Glitch, and his scowl deepened. He let out a short croak. The other Barash bowed again and gestured toward Glitch and the others.

Glitch leaned toward Nen as the Barash chattered, chirping and trilling.

"What's it saying?" he whispered.

"That is Melian—the Lorock's daughter. Melian is insisting that you be allowed a trial."

"With a judge? That sounds better than summary

execution."

Nen frowned and shook his head. "No, you must perform a trial. If you survive, you will be released back to the wild."

Glitch ran his fingers through his hair. He'd never been very good at tests. "Still better than summary execution, I guess."

Nen looked at Glitch. He didn't look convinced.

Melian had finished talking and was waiting while the Lorock conferred with the Barash who'd brought him the sword. As they talked, the sword-bearer glared at Glitch. It clearly liked a good sacrifice and didn't want to be denied. Around the platform, the Barash waited patiently, watching the events unfold.

Eventually, the Lorock nodded toward Melian. A ripple of excitement spread through the crowd. Melian turned to Glitch, wings rustling. She gestured to the guards standing behind them. They stepped forward and pulled Glitch and the others roughly to their feet. Melian pointed at Nen and chirped twice.

Nen bowed slightly. "Melian wants me to turn her words for you."

Melian chirped. Her voice was soft, a marked contrast to the harshness of the Lorock's.

Nen listened while Melian spoke then translated for Glitch. "In the Lorock's infinite and merciful generosity, our wisest one has decided that you should undergo the trial of the fallen. If you pass, you will be allowed to go free unharmed."

"What do we have to do in this trial?" said Anderson.

Nen translated the question into the Barash's staccato language, speaking aloud rather than through telepathy. Melian turned to Anderson and regarded her for a moment before replying.

"Melian says you may choose. Trial by fire. Trial by earth. Trial by liquid," said Nen.

"Shouldn't that be earth, wind, and fire?" asked Glitch.

Anderson ignored him. "And if we refuse?"

Melian listened to Nen repeat the question then gestured toward the sword in the Lorock's hands.

"It doesn't seem like we have much choice," said the doctor.

Glitch nodded toward Melian. She bowed her head slightly then spread her arms wide. Her wings extended behind her, the feathers a wall of shimmering color.

Melian let out a long screech, followed by a dozen rapid clicks. The excitement of the crowd grew. The Barash stamped their feet, flapped their wings, let loose rough, guttural cries. The noise echoed around the trees, reminding Glitch of a planet full of apes rather than a race of bird-people.

As the noise died down, a gap opened in the crowd, and Melian gestured for them to follow her. She led them across the platform to a wide walkway. As they passed, the Barash unfurled their wings and lifted gracefully into the air. Under different circumstances, Glitch might have found the sight awe inspiring. As it was, it was simply terrifying.

The walkway creaked and rocked as they traveled across it. Barash flew past them, dipping underneath the walkway one moment, swooping overhead the next. Glitch spotted the Lorock gliding ahead of them. He landed on another broad platform at the end of the walkway and stood, watching impassively.

When they reached the platform, Melian gestured to them to wait. This one was also built around the trunk of a tree. It wasn't as big as the first, but it was impressive in its own right.

A wide shelf was attached to the tree. Three clay urns sat on the shelf, each one sealed with a wooden stopper. One was marked with a brown circle, another a red triangle, and the last with a white symbol that looked like an S laid on its side.

Melian joined the Lorock, and they walked across the platform. They stood on either side of the shelf and faced Glitch and the others. Most of the crowd had followed them across the gap, but instead of standing on the platform, they landed in nearby trees or stayed on the walkways. Other than the Lorock and Melian, the platform itself was free of Barash.

"This must be a sacred place," said Zheng, sounding intrigued. "Or at least special in some way."

"Hopefully it's special in a 'let us get out of here alive' kind of way," said Glitch.

Anderson didn't join in the conversation, but Glitch saw her scanning the platform and the trees around it, looking for an opportunity to escape. Given her concerned expression, she evidently hadn't found one.

There was movement behind them, and the sword bearer landed on the platform. It shook its wings twice then bowed deeply to Melian and the Lorock. The Lorock made a long whistling sound that rose and fell in pitch. The sword bearer bowed again then walked over to the shelf.

"Now you must choose," said Nen. "Fire, earth, or liquid."

"Any preferences?" said Glitch.

"I don't like the sound of fire," said Anderson. "But other than that, your guess is as good as mine."

"I concur," said Zheng.

"Nen? Any ideas?" said Glitch.

Nen shook his head.

"Okay," said Glitch. "Here goes. Eeny, meeny, mincy, moe. Catch a Klingon by the toe. If he punches, let him go. Eeny, meeny, miney, moe."

"Catch a Klingon?" said Anderson.

Glitch shrugged. "Liquid. Tell her liquid."

Nen made three low-pitched clicks, and the sword bearer removed the urn marked with white squiggles. It treated it with great reverence, holding it with just the tips of its fingers as it walked toward them.

"What's in there, Nen?" asked Glitch.

"They call it… God's Essence."

Glitch glanced at Nen, eyebrows raised. The So-lang had moved a couple of feet away, trying to distance himself from Glitch and the others. He looked terrified.

Glitch thought for a moment then stepped forward and held out his hand. "Wait. Please."

The sword—now urn-bearer stopped. Melian raised her eyebrows in a look of amused surprise. The Lorock just looked angry.

Glitch swallowed, suddenly very cold in the chill morning air. "Nen has nothing to do with this. He just happened to be in my… cage… cell… whatever."

Nen hissed quietly and backed away farther.

"Translate that for me," said Glitch, waving between Nen and the Barash carrying the urn.

Nen shook his head rapidly.

The doctor stepped forward and pointed at Nen. "He is not," she said, raising her voice and shaking her head, "with us." She pointed at herself and shook her head then repeated the action, pointing at Nen.

The Barash carrying the urn tilted its head then turned toward the Lorock for guidance. The Lorock stared at the doctor. His eyes narrowed, angry, and it wasn't hard for Glitch to imagine him swooping across the platform, slamming into the doctor, and knocking her into the forest below. The image of the young So-lang falling through the trees flashed through his mind, and he shuddered.

The Lorock nodded. Melian spoke, and Nen moved farther away, nodding and bowing with evident relief.

Zheng bowed low. "Thank you."

The Lorock looked unimpressed and gestured impatiently toward the Barash carrying the urn. The urn-bearer bowed and walked the rest of the way to Glitch. It pointed at the urn, then at Glitch, then Doctor Zheng, then Anderson.

"I guess it wants us to drink from the urn," said Glitch, trying to mask the fear in his voice.

"It certainly looks that way," said the doctor.

"And I'm supposed to go first."

"Uh huh," said Anderson.

"In that case… unless anyone's got any better ideas… that's what I'm going to do…"

When neither Anderson nor Doctor Zheng said anything, Glitch took the urn. It was heavy.

The Barash carefully removed the wooden stopper. Whatever was inside sloshed around as Glitch raised the urn toward his nose. It smelled sweet with a hint of cinnamon and reminded him of the cinnamon rolls he bought from his local baker. Suddenly he was intensely homesick. He really shouldn't have entered that competition.

The Barash's wings twitched. It hissed and made a drinking motion with its hand.

Glitch took a deep breath. "If you have a plan, Captain… now would be the time."

Anderson didn't respond.

"Okay… here goes." Glitch raised the urn to his mouth.

He took a sip. The liquid was thin and slightly oily, but it was so sweet it set his teeth on edge. He began to lower the urn, but the Barash tipped it back.

Liquid flooded Glitch's mouth, and some of it dribbled out of the side. He suspected spitting out their holy beverage wouldn't go down too well, so he swallowed. The liquid slipped down easily, coating his throat and leaving a thin layer around his mouth. He ran his tongue over his teeth, trying to wipe them clean.

The Barash watched Glitch intently then took the urn back.

Glitch looked around, waiting for something to happen.

"How do you feel?" said Doctor Zheng.

Glitch shrugged. "Fine. It's just very sweet water."

The urn-bearer, apparently satisfied, moved to Doctor Zheng and gave her the urn.

She grabbed it, took a deep swig, and handed it back to the Barash. She grimaced and swallowed. "I thought you said it was sweet? That tasted like liquefied jalapenos."

"It was sweet when I drank it."

Doctor Zheng scowled and coughed, tears forming at the corners of her eyes. The Barash watched Zheng for a while, just as it had Glitch, then walked over to Anderson. Glitch thought he could see a hint of amusement on the Barash's face, but it was hard to tell.

Anderson regarded the urn with suspicion. The Barash shook it toward her and gave a couple of agitated clicks. Anderson took the urn, sniffed it, then poured some of the liquid into her mouth. Glitch held his breath. He was convinced this was all some sort of practical joke and she too would get the jalapeno juice and hate him for it.

Anderson squeezed her eyes shut as she swallowed.

She opened her eyes again. "It tasted like lemons to me."

"Interesting," said the doctor. "I wonder what it is."

"Nen said it's God's Essence," said Glitch.

Doctor Zheng looked at Glitch, one eyebrow raised.

Glitch shrugged. "I guess they're not atheists."

The Barash retrieved the urn from Anderson, bowed to the Lorock, and moved to the side of the platform. Glitch looked around at the Barash. They were all watching and waiting, the air filled with expectation.

"Did we pass?" said Glitch.

"I... don't know," said Anderson.

Glitch opened his mouth to ask Nen what was supposed to happen next, but before he could speak, an express train of pain tore through his stomach. He felt as if someone had hit him with a wooden plank covered in rusty nails. He crumpled, screaming. Tendrils of pain wove through his body, setting nerve endings alight as though the nails had brought with them thousands of fire ants swarming across his skin, biting and stinging.

Adrenaline flooded his system. His heart quickened. He raked his nails down his arms, trying to tear away whatever was burning his flesh. Glitch's spine contracted, snapping him backward until he was lying on the ground, screaming. His right leg cramped up, then twitched. It shuddered and shook, his heel rapping out a rhythm on the wooden platform. Wave after wave of agony washed over him. A metal band wrapped around his chest, constricting his breathing.

Glitch lay on the floor, gasping for breath, clutching at himself as darkness swept over him.

CHAPTER SEVENTEEN
A Deadly Drink

Glitch, Anderson, and Doctor Zheng are saved from ritual execution by the Barash, Melian. In exchange, the humans agree to undergo a trial. They choose trial by liquid, and each of them takes a drink from an urn containing "God's Essence." Glitch tastes sweet water, but Doctor Zheng's drink tastes like "liquefied jalapenos" and Captain Anderson's is sour like lemons. Anderson and Zheng are unaffected by the drink, but a vicious pain tears through Glitch's stomach.

Glitch fell to the floor, screaming. His arms itched and burned as though thousands of fire ants were swarming over his body. Adrenaline flooded his system. His heart quickened. He raked his nails down his arms, trying to tear away whatever was burning his flesh.

Glitch's spine contracted, bending him backward until he was lying on his back, screaming. His right leg cramped up then twitched. It shuddered and shook, his heel rapping out a rhythm on the wooden platform. Again and again, agony washed over him. A metal band wrapped around his chest, constricting his breathing. Darkness took him.

Glitch floated in the blackness. The pain was gone, replaced by an all-encompassing numbness. Part of him welcomed it, embraced it, grasped at it as a way to escape the humiliation life so often sent his way. But that part of him was small, a tiny sliver of a multifaceted personality. The rest of him fought. Fought to drag him out of the blackness. Fought to find the light that he'd been told existed—the light that would bring him back to Anderson and Zheng, to Kalith and Nen. He wanted to see everyone again. All of them. Even the Barash.

Glitch tasted something bitter, sudden and unexpected, a beacon of sensation in the blackness, and he opened his eyes.

Nen was bent over him, his broad hands pressed to Glitch's lips. He was forcing something into Glitch's mouth, a paste, bitter and grassy. Glitch twisted his head away, but Nen pulled it back. "Eat."

Anderson appeared behind Nen, staring at Glitch. Her forehead was creased with worry and, for reasons he couldn't quite grasp, that made Glitch happy.

"You've been poisoned," she said. "Nen has an antidote."

Glitch grimaced and swallowed the bitter paste, forcing it down. "Water?" His voice was dry, rasping.

Anderson looked around. "Please, help him. Get some water."

It took Glitch a few seconds to remember who she was talking to. Then images of Melian and the other Barash came flooding back. They'd been undergoing a test, a trial.

Glitch tried to push himself upright, but Nen held him down. "Be still."

Anderson reappeared. The emerald canopy behind her head reminded Glitch of a green-screen movie set. A wave of nausea rolled through his body, and his vision blurred.

"Stay with us," said Anderson, pressing her hand against his forehead.

Glitch wondered if she'd brought him water. The world dimmed.

When Glitch opened his eyes again, he was back in the cage. He was propped up against its side, Anderson kneeling beside him.

She uncorked a leather pouch and held it to Glitch's mouth. "Drink."

Glitch let the cool liquid fill his mouth. If the gods had a nectar, he imagined that was what it might taste like. He swallowed. "Thank you."

"How do you feel?" asked Anderson.

"I'm fine." Glitch felt dizzy and had a vaguely unpleasant tingling in his mouth, but otherwise, he did actually feel fine. "What happened? I remember the trial. I drank something from a clay urn, but that's about it."

"It was God's Essence—at least, that's what the Barash call it. The doctor and I drank some as well. We're okay, but you had some sort of allergic reaction and… passed out. Nen scraped some moss from one of the trees and gave it to you."

Doctor Zheng appeared beside Anderson. "He saved your life."

"Saved it? You mean I would have died?"

"No, you *were* dead," said the doctor.

Glitch's mouth fell open. "I died? I thought I just passed out."

Anderson glared at Zheng. "I was trying to be discreet."

Glitch ran his fingers through his hair, breathing heavily.

"You'll be fine," said the doctor. "Nen gave you the antidote."

"No." It was Nen. He was standing at the edge of the cage, his face dark. "It was not an… antidote."

"What do you mean?" said Anderson.

"The moss only eases the effects of the God's Essence. It does not cure."

"So I'm still going to die?"

Nen lowered his head.

Glitch stared at the ground. If he hadn't already been sitting down, he'd have collapsed. "How long do I have to live?"

"I do not know, but… less than a day."

"So I've gone all Dennis Quaid," said Glitch.

"Except you know who killed you," said Anderson.

Doctor Zheng raised her eyebrows at Anderson. She

mouthed "film," and the doctor nodded.

"There must be something we can do," said Anderson.

Nen shook his head. "Once the God's Essence has a hold over you, there is no release, only death."

"But why didn't it affect us?" said the doctor.

"God saw fit to save you."

Cursing, Anderson stood and stormed across the cage, fists clenched, looking for something to punch. Eventually she settled on slamming her hand against the wooden bars in frustration.

"Don't worry," said the doctor. "We'll get you back to Earth and find a cure."

Glitch raised his head then gestured around the cage. "We'll need to get out of here first."

Doctor Zheng crouched beside him and placed a hand on his shoulder. "We will."

There was unexpected warmth in Zheng's voice, and Glitch forced a smile. Then he looked across at Anderson, and her defeated expression told him all he needed to know.

He lifted the waterskin and took another sip. This time the water tasted musty, ordinary. It wasn't what he'd choose as a last drink—he was more of a Jack Daniel's kind of guy—but it would do. A quiet calm settled over him. He was surprised. If someone had asked him what he'd do if he found out he only had a few hours left to live, he'd have said he'd rant and rave, throw things, curse God and everyone around him. He didn't picture himself as the sort of person who'd jump directly to acceptance.

Maybe he was still in the denial phase and anger would come later.

He raised the pouch to his lips to take another drink when Anderson called across the cage. "What's that?"

She was pointing through the bars at the ground. A dozen dark shapes moved through the forest beneath them. They looked like people, or people's shadows at least.

Nen stiffened. "Hunters."

There was a high-pitched whine, and a bolt of blue light, about three feet long, flew from the ground and slammed into a nearby tree. Instantly, the wood caught fire. Blue flames wrapped around the trunk. Wood crackled and spat.

Somewhere off in the distance, a horn sounded, closely followed by another. A third joined it, this one nearby. Barash swarmed from the trees. Some dived toward the ground while others fled into the canopy. Two more bolts flew into the trees. One of them smashed through a walkway, shattering it. The other hit one of the Barash square in the chest. It burst into flames and fell screaming to the ground.

There was a flash of blue as another tree, this one on the other side of the village, caught fire. One of the bolts roared by, inches from hitting Glitch's cage. He could feel the heat of the fire as it passed. Or he imagined he could.

Screams echoed through the trees as again and again, the hunters fired at the village. More of them appeared, at least twenty that Glitch could see, and untold numbers could be hidden within the undergrowth. He still couldn't make out any details beyond a vaguely humanoid shape. They were just shadows darting among the trees. Glitch wondered if it was the Invisitude.

Some of the Barash had reached the ground and were fighting the hunters. They were losing. Their swords and spears were no match for the hunters' energy weapons. One by one, the Barash fell to the ground. Even those who managed to get in close enough to fight hand to hand were quickly overwhelmed by sheer numbers. Glitch saw one of them caught, wrapped in heavy netting, then knocked unconscious. Two of the shadowy hunters dragged it off into the undergrowth.

Their cage shook as a Barash landed on top of it. It was carrying a small Barash child who was crying and making a plaintive chirping sound. The Barash brushed its head as it looked around, searching for something or someone. A streak of blue flashed past, and the Barash kicked off, launching into the canopy and out of sight.

"Who are they?" shouted Anderson, pointing toward the shadows swarming through the undergrowth.

"Relorians," shouted Nen. "They hunt for sport, to show how powerful they are."

With another burst of blue light, a nearby tree exploded into flame. The fire was spreading, leaping from tree to tree. Gray smoke hung around the village, obscuring their view. Most of the Barash were gone, either killed or captured or escaped, but the hunters kept firing until the entire village was ablaze. Flames flickered in nearby trees, jumping from branch to branch, spreading rapidly toward the cage containing Glitch and the others.

Glitch saw the shot a fraction of a second before it hit their cage, a thin blue smudge rushing toward them. It slammed into the tree in a blaze of blue light that hurt his eyes and showered them with fragments of burning wood. Clouds of smoke filled the cage. The cage shuddered and listed to the left. There was a creaking sound, and a lump of burning wood fell from the ceiling.

"We can get out," said Glitch, pointing.

The impact had opened up a hole in the cage near the actual door. The edges were burning, and the fire was spreading quickly, but there was enough room for them to escape. If they were quick.

Glitch ran to the cage wall. "Come on."

Doctor Zheng got there first. She jumped up, grabbed the wooden bars, and began to climb. The cage rocked ominously. Anderson followed her up. Nen stood at the bottom of the cage, looking nervously at the blue flames flickering above him.

"There's no time," said Glitch. "You have to go now."

The cage shuddered, and Nen shook his head. He stepped backward.

Glitch leaned toward him, his eyes blazing. "If you stay here, you'll die."

Nen swallowed then ran to the side of the cage and climbed up. Glitch gave Nen a few seconds' head start then followed him. Chunks of burning wood dropped from the roof. The floor of the cage was starting to smolder. At least the firing seemed to have stopped. Perhaps they would get out of this alive after all.

As Anderson got to the opening, the ground shook, and the air filled with a low rumbling. The cage shifted again, pitching to the right. Nen yelled in terror, clinging to the bars. Doctor Zheng's feet slipped, leaving her hanging from the roof of the cage. Glitch hooked one leg around the wooden bars to stop himself from falling. The smoke was getting in his eyes, making them stream. He could hardly see where he was.

Doctor Zheng swung her legs back toward the bars of the cage. Her hand slipped, and she screamed.

"I'm coming to get you," shouted Glitch. Coughing, he started climbing toward the doctor.

There was a cracking sound and a cascade of sparks and fire. Burning wood fell from the top of the cage as the ropes supporting it gave way.

A moment later, the cage fell.

CHAPTER EIGHTEEN
Human Prey

The So-lang Nen gives Glitch an antidote to the poison, but although it will buy him some time, Glitch will eventually die. As Glitch considers his fate, the Barash village is attacked by a group of Relorian hunters. Their energy weapons set fire to the Barash village, and Glitch, Anderson, Zheng, and Nen are trapped as the flames close in. A blast from a Relorian weapon hits the cage, opening a hole in the roof, and they climb toward it.

As Anderson reached the opening, the ground shook. The cage shifted to the right. Nen yelled in terror, hands clamped around the bars.

Doctor Zheng slipped and ended up hanging from the roof of the cage. Glitch hooked a leg around the bars to stop himself from falling. The air was filled with smoke, and his eyes were streaming. Doctor Zheng tried to swing back toward the side of the cage, but her hand slipped. She screamed.

"I'm coming to get you," shouted Glitch, and he climbed up to the doctor.

There was a cracking sound and a shower of sparks, and fire and burning wood fell from the top of the cage as the ropes supporting it gave way.

A moment later, the cage fell.

Wood splintered and cracked as the cage crashed through branch after branch. Glitch clung to the wooden bars, trying to avoid being thrown loose as he was bounced around. The ball-like cage collided with a thick branch, and the right-hand side folded inward. Two of the bars shattered, creating a pair of lethal-looking spikes. A lump of burning wood bounced past Anderson, narrowly missing her head.

The cage rolled sideways, dropped a couple of feet, then hit another branch. Glitch twisted away as a ragged spike of wood the size of his arm burst through the bars near his head. The cage held steady for a moment, resting on top of a thick branch, then tipped slowly off the side and fell the last twenty feet to the ground.

The cage's shell took most of the impact, shattering into a cloud of wood and dirt and leaves. Glitch landed on his shoulder, the impact sending pain ripping through his body.

The others landed around him and lay there, groaning. Glitch stared up through the remains of the cage. He could see clusters of flames dotted throughout the trees and a clear path where they'd crashed through the canopy.

Glitch was the first to move. He rolled onto his side

then brought himself up into a crouch. Tentatively, he checked himself for injuries. He'd gathered a few more bruises during the descent, but otherwise he was okay. The forest seemed empty, but sounds of movement came from off to the right. It wouldn't be long before the hunters came to find out what had happened to their prey. Glitch didn't want to be there when they arrived.

Doctor Zheng was lying facedown nearby, but Glitch saw her moving. He hurried over and placed a hand on her shoulder.

"Are you okay?" he whispered.

"In a manner of speaking," said the doctor. She rolled over. There was a cut on her forehead and she looked a little pale, but otherwise she seemed okay.

"Anything broken?" said Glitch.

"I don't think so, just a few bruises. Check the others."

Glitch walked over to Anderson, and she gave him a halfhearted smile.

"That was a hell of a ride," said Anderson. "I'd rather not go on it again if it's okay, though."

"You've got a deal," said Glitch.

Glitch held out a hand and helped Anderson to her feet. A sharp pain drilled into Glitch's stomach, and a wave of dizziness washed over him. He stepped forward, realized he was about to grab Anderson, tried not to, and staggered sideways, almost falling over.

Anderson steadied him. "Are you okay?"

Glitch clutched at his stomach. The pain was already fading, taking the dizziness with it. He nodded.

Nen was lying on the ground a few feet away, his left arm twisted awkwardly beneath him. He wasn't moving, and his eyes were closed.

Anderson glanced around the forest then crouched next to him. "Nen?"

Nen groaned and opened his eyes. "My arm…" His shoulder blade was jutting out at an awkward angle. At the very least it was dislocated, probably broken.

"Can you move?" asked Anderson.

Nen nodded, wincing, then rolled to his side. He let out a cry and grabbed his wrist. His face distorted in pain, he carefully pulled his arm against his chest.

"Shhh," hissed Anderson, looking around. "Try not to make too much noise."

Nen nodded.

"Doctor?" said Anderson. "Can you take a look at this?"

Doctor Zheng was sitting up now and had her hand pressed against the cut on her forehead. She nodded and carefully got to her feet. Anderson and Glitch stood watch, scanning the forest for signs of life while the doctor checked Nen's shoulder. Faint shouts drifted through the trees, but that was all. If any of the other prisoners had escaped, there was no sign of them.

"I don't think it's broken," said the doctor, "but it is dislocated."

"Can you fix it?" said Nen.

"Yes, but it won't be pleasant."

"Please, do what you need to."

Doctor Zheng retrieved a piece of wood from the ground and gave it to Nen. "Bite down on this."

Glitch turned away, not wanting to watch. He should have covered his ears as well, because the soft cracking sound he heard a few moments later made his stomach lurch. Nen let out a cry, muffled by the wood in his mouth.

Zheng tore some vines from a nearby tree and jury-rigged a sling. Nen still looked in pain, but he was already sitting up when they heard a chorus of rough shouts, the words unintelligible.

"We have to go," said Glitch.

"But go where?" said Doctor Zheng.

Nen struggled to his feet. "There are tunnels nearby. We should be safe there."

Glitch helped the So-lang up.

Nen looked around, getting his bearings, then pointed off to the right. "They should be that way."

He picked his way across the wreckage of the cage, but he stumbled. Glitch ran forward, slipping his arm under the So-lang's shoulders to support him.

There was a high-pitched whine as something passed overhead. Glitch tried to find the source of the noise through the trees, but the foliage was too thick. Behind them, the voices grew louder. They hadn't been spotted, but it was just a matter of time.

They moved through the forest as quickly as they could, but there was no trail and it was slow going. Nen had to stop twice to ease his injured arm and find his bearings. Glitch had no idea how they'd find the tunnels. As far as he could tell, there were no landmarks, and every tree looked almost identical.

Nen grimaced as they forced their way through a waist-high line of thorny bushes into a clearing. "They should be…"

Wood cracked behind them. Glitch turned and peered between the trees. Three shadowy figures were moving rapidly toward them.

"Now would be a really good time to find those tunnels," said Glitch.

Nen pointed across the clearing toward a pair of thin trees surrounded by more of the thick bushes. "There."

They hurried across the clearing and circled the trees. There was a low cave, almost completely obscured by vegetation. Glitch ducked out of sight as two Relorians moved into the clearing.

"Go on," he whispered, "help Nen."

Anderson pushed her way through the bushes, holding back the thick branches so that Nen could get through. He had to crawl on his hands and knees to get into the cave. The pain from his arm was clear on his face as he crawled out of sight.

Glitch crouched behind the bushes, keeping watch as Anderson and Doctor Zheng followed Nen. He could make out the dark shapes moving steadily across the clearing. Both of them were identical, at least seven feet tall, and much thinner than a human. Their bodies shifted and swirled as though they were made from smoke instead of flesh, and their eyes were blue sparks suspended in the cloud of gray.

As Zheng disappeared into the cave and Glitch prepared to follow her, one of the creatures turned toward Glitch. Glitch froze, too terrified to move in case he gave himself away. The blue eyes stared right at him, boring through the undergrowth and into his flesh. He felt them penetrating his soul, pinning it down and laying it bare. It was all he could do not to turn and run into the forest. Sweat trickled down Glitch's back. His throat turned dry, and he felt a cough building inside him. Then the hunter turned away, and Glitch could breathe again.

Glitch pushed through the bushes. He tried to be as quiet as possible, but still the branches seemed so loud, he thought the entire forest must be able to hear him. He dropped to his knees and crawled into the cave. A few feet inside, the tunnel opened up. Glitch crawled straight into Doctor Zheng as she stood waiting for him.

"Sorry, Doctor. Where are they?"

The doctor didn't reply, but a phosphorescent light appeared a few feet down the tunnel. Anderson and Nen were holding one of the glowing sticks Glitch had seen in the So-lang village.

"We must go," said Nen.

Glitch heard the pain in Nen's voice. He hurried down the tunnel toward the So-lang. The doctor followed close behind.

Anderson gave them both a glow stick, and they walked. Almost immediately the tunnel split into three.

They took the leftmost branch, ducking past a tangle of roots hanging from the ceiling. A few feet farther, the tunnel split into two. They took the right path this time and began to descend a gradual slope.

Again and again the tunnels split, but Nen appeared to know exactly where he was going. At first, Glitch strained for sounds of pursuit, but he quickly realized that Nen had chosen their escape route well. No one would be able to find them in the maze of tunnels. They must run for miles beneath the forest. The walls were a rich, dark brown, damp to the touch, but after half an hour or so, they took on a reddish tinge and became dry and dusty.

When they finally stopped to let Nen rest, Glitch pointed at the walls. "Are we under the desert now?"

"The plains. Yes." Nen was leaning against the wall, eyes closed, beads of sweat scattered across his bald head.

"Nen," said Glitch, "we need to get to the silver city."

"Why?" asked Nen.

"We need to find the way home."

"Home?"

"It's a place called Earth."

Nen frowned and pointed toward the ground. "Earth?"

"Well... yes."

"Our planet may be in danger," said Anderson. "We need to warn our government, our leaders. But we can't do that unless we get to the city. Can you help?"

Nen nodded. Wiping his brow, he crouched down. He leaned on his uninjured arm, digging his hand into the earth. The ground was packed hard, but Nen's hand slipped into it as if it was sand. The earth around his wrist moved, shifting and undulating. It looked as if dozens of worms were trying to break through to the surface.

Gradually the moving earth aligned into a series of thin ridges, stretching away from Nen's hand. The ridges shifted and twisted then broke away and moved off down the corridor, leaving a thin trail of displaced earth in their wake. Nen pulled his hand from the ground and gingerly wiped the dirt off it. Fresh beads of sweat had formed on his brow.

He leaned back against the dusty wall. "My brothers will be here soon. They will take you to the city. I wish I could help you myself, but my arm…"

"What about the hunters, the Relorians?" said Glitch.

"I do not think they will have tried to follow us this far."

"But wouldn't humans be a great prize for a hunter?" said Glitch. "Like in *Predator?*"

"I… I do not understand," said Nen.

"It's a story," said Anderson.

"A legend?"

Glitch laughed. "Sort of, yes."

Anderson stifled a smile. Doctor Zheng tutted.

"The Relorians weren't looking for us. They came for the Barash. They are more of a challenge. There would be no prestige in acquiring you and me. After all, we've already been captured—how intelligent can we be?"

Glitch felt more than a little insulted and was about to object when the doctor cut him off. "Will you be okay?

Your arm, I mean. Will it heal?"

Nen nodded. "The healers will repair the damage. We are quite resilient."

Doctor Zheng didn't seem convinced, but she didn't say anything more. Nen closed his eyes and tipped his head back against the wall. Glitch wished they'd thought to pick up a couple of pouches of water. He was parched.

It took almost an hour for the So-lang to appear. There were four of them—two males and two females. Glitch didn't recognize any of them from the village.

They eyed the humans warily then hurried past them to Nen. The So-lang barely made a sound as they moved. Glitch couldn't help but think that if they'd had malicious intentions, the So-lang could have killed him, Anderson, and Zheng before they realized they were in any danger. The two males knelt beside Nen while the females stood between him and the humans, watching them suspiciously.

Each of the So-lang carried a square leather bag. The one nearest Nen reached inside his, removed a carved wooden gourd, and handed it to Nen, who opened it and took a long, eager drink. Nen returned the gourd to the So-lang, and he pulled a glass jar filled with thick white jelly from the bag. He removed the wooden stopper from the jar and dipped his hands inside. He scooped out two handfuls of the white substance then carefully held Nen's arm. Nen barely flinched as the man rubbed his hands over Nen's shoulder. Glitch was surprised Nen wasn't screaming in agony. If anything, he seemed relaxed, comfortable.

Once most of the jelly had soaked into Nen's skin, the So-lang rubbed the remainder into his own legs and stood. Another So-lang helped Nen to his feet. Nen still held his arm awkwardly, trying not to move it, but it didn't seem to bother him as much as it had been.

The two female So-lang turned toward Nen. He gestured toward Glitch and the others with his good hand and made a few hissing, clicking noises. The female So-lang replied, and the conversation went back and forth a few times. Eventually, there was a pause. One of the female So-lang turned toward Glitch, regarding him with clear suspicion. Glitch tried smiling, but the effort went unrewarded.

The other female So-lang seemed less bothered by the presence of the humans, and after a brief exchange with Nen, she turned to them. "My name is Kel. This is Aro. Nen has asked us to lead you to the outskirts of the Unnamed city so that you may find a way home. It is not far, but we should leave now."

"Thank you," said Doctor Zheng. "We are very grateful."

Glitch coughed lightly and made a dry rasping sound in the back of his throat.

"Very subtle," whispered Anderson. Louder, she said, "I don't want to stretch your hospitality too far, but do you have any water you can spare?"

Kel looked genuinely horrified. "Oh please, forgive me. Of course. We were so concerned with Nen, we forgot our manners."

She waved toward Aro, who let out a clearly audible tut and reached into her bag. She brought out another wooden gourd and, reluctantly, handed it to Anderson.

"Thank you." Anderson pulled the stopper from the gourd and took a quick drink. She swilled the water around her mouth before swallowing. As she handed the container to Doctor Zheng, she gave a slight nod.

Glitch wondered whether he should have been the one to try the water first; after all, he'd already been poisoned. The thought brought an uncomfortable sensation to his stomach that he hoped was just his imagination.

The doctor took a couple of sips then handed the gourd to Glitch. The water inside was cool and fresh with no sign of the mustiness of the water the Barash had given them. Glitch eagerly took a drink then offered it to Aro. She shook her head and refused to take it. Glitch's stomach gurgled, and she grimaced, looking at Kel with a disgusted look. Glitch blushed.

Ignoring Anderson's smile, Glitch walked over to Nen. "Thank you. You saved my life. I'm sorry you got hurt."

Nen frowned and shook his head. "No, I must thank you. I would have died at the hands of the Barash or the hunters if it were not for you."

"I guess that makes us even."

Nen smiled and reached down to his belt. He pulled off a small leather pouch and handed it to Glitch. "If you feel the pain returning, eat a pinch of this moss. It will give you some more time. Perhaps you can find a cure on your own planet."

"I'm sure I will. Thank you."

Glitch offered his hand then waved it in a halfhearted high-five motion before returning it to his side. Nen frowned. Glitch settled for another thank-you and moved away.

Anderson shook her head, a slight smile playing across her lips. She walked over to Nen and gave him a gentle hug. He seemed surprised and unsure what to do, but she held on long enough for him to wrap his good arm around her in return.

"Take care of yourself," she said once she'd released him. "Don't get caught again."

Nen shook his head, his face serious. "I won't."

"And take care of that arm," said Doctor Zheng. "I don't want to have to come back here to sort it out again."

Nen's eyes grew wide, and he shook his head sharply.

"We're ready whenever you are," said Anderson, stifling a laugh.

Kel smiled and walked toward a narrow tunnel leading off to the right. She pulled a short stick from her bag and scraped it down the wall. The stick began to glow, the soft white light illuminating the caves around them. Kel said something to Aro, and she reluctantly pulled out her own glow stick and lit it.

"This way," said Kel.

Glitch, Anderson, and Zheng followed Kel. Glitch nodded toward the two male So-lang as he left. They tipped their heads in acknowledgment but said nothing.

They walked in silence through the tunnels. There were fewer branches now, but they still reached a junction every few minutes. Like Nen, Kel seemed to know instinctively which direction they should go. The only real choice they had was to trust her—there didn't seem to be any way to get to the surface. Glitch had hoped Aro might stay with Nen, but she didn't. Instead she followed them, a quietly bubbling mass of resentment. Glitch was right in front of her, and he could feel her watching him.

As Kel led them through the tunnels, the walls around them changed from red earth to a denser clay-like material and finally to red rock. Much to Aro's disgust, they stopped three times for the humans to rest and take a few sips of water. The fourth time they stopped, it was next to a narrow crack in the wall.

"This is as far as we can take you," said Kel. "The entrance to the caves beneath the city is through there. We... cannot enter them."

Doctor Zheng clasped Kel's hands. "You have already done so much for us, thank you."

"Yes, thank you," said Anderson.

Kel smiled and shook her head. "Cana-Nen would not be alive today if it were not for you."

"He saved my life, too," said Glitch, patting the pouch of moss.

Kel gave a slight bow. There was a distant rumbling, and the ground shook slightly beneath their feet. Aro looked at the ceiling and hissed twice.

Kel handed Anderson one of the glowing sticks. "We

must go. Good luck on your journey."

Without waiting for a reply, the So-lang hurried back down the tunnel, disappearing into the darkness. There was another rumble, louder this time, nearer. The ground shook again.

Anderson held up the glow stick and peered into the crack in the wall. "There's a cave. Wait here until I call you."

Turning sideways, she squeezed through the opening and out of sight. A couple of minutes later, she called to Glitch and the doctor, and they followed her through the gap into a small, nondescript cave. A gateway was set into one wall. It shimmered in the glow of the phosphorescent globes clinging to the walls around it.

Doctor Zheng walked over to the gateway.

"Hold on. We don't know where it leads," said Glitch. "It could go anywhere."

"He's right," said Anderson.

"There's only one way to find out," said the doctor, and she stepped into the gateway.

"Dammit!" said Anderson. "Come on."

She ran across the cave and through the gateway. Glitch took a deep breath, wished yet again that he hadn't entered that damn competition, and followed her.

It took Glitch a few seconds to gather his thoughts and shake off the chill once he'd exited the gateway. Light and noise assaulted his senses, and thick clouds of smoke obscured his view. The Invisitude city had become a war zone.

CHAPTER NINETEEN
Countdown to Disaster

Glitch, Anderson, Doctor Zheng, and Nen are trapped in a prison cage suspended high in a treetop village when a group of Relorian hunters attacks. During the battle, their cage is hit and falls from the tree, crashing to the ground. Nen is injured, but the four manage to escape the Relorians and reach a network of underground tunnels. Nen calls for help, and four So-lang arrive. Two remain with the injured Nen while the others lead the humans through the tunnels to a gateway that will take them back to the Invisitude city.

Doctor Zheng walked toward the gateway.

"Hold on," said Glitch. "We don't know where it leads. It could go anywhere."

"He's right," said Anderson.

"There's only one way to find out," said Zheng, and she stepped through the gateway.

"Dammit!" said Anderson. "Come on."

Anderson ran to the gateway and stepped through.

Glitch took a deep breath, wished yet again that he hadn't entered the damn competition, and followed Anderson.

Once he was on the other side, it took Glitch a few seconds to shake off the chill of the journey and gather his thoughts. Light and noise assaulted his senses, and thick clouds of smoke obscured the view around him. The Invisitude city had become a war zone.

Smoke and heat from the fires that blazed across the city filled the air. Something exploded nearby, the concussion sending fresh clouds of dust and smoke billowing down the street. The ground lurched, tipping Glitch forward. His eyes streamed, the tears almost blinding him. Rubbing his arm across his eyes to clear them, he searched the street for signs of Anderson and Zheng.

They were sheltered behind a twisted sheet of metal, the tattered remains of a small rectangular building. Whatever it had been before, all that was left was a pile of bent and torn metal and a rat's nest of twisted bars and cables. Sparks burst from the tips of the cables and bounced, crackling, across the floor.

Glitch ran over to the barricade and crouched beside Anderson. "What the hell is going on?"

Anderson shook her head. "I don't know."

"Why didn't we just stay in the cave?" said Glitch. "The cave was safe."

With a loud pop, a jet of steam broke through the ground a few feet away. Glitch flinched, covering his face against the sudden wave of heat. The ground shook, dislodging a sheet of metal from the building opposite. It slammed into the ground with a clang. Somewhere off in the distance, a siren wailed briefly then died.

A breeze swept down the street, clearing the smoke for an instant, and Glitch looked across the city. Pillars of smoke rose from dozens of buildings. Pockets of blue fire burned brightly, the heat haze around them distorting the air. There was no sign of whoever was doing this, but there was a blue flash of another explosion. Glitch thought of the Relorians.

Doctor Zheng pointed across the street. "Look."

Kalith was standing next to a small hexagonal building, waving to them. They ran to her, crouched low like journalists in a war zone.

"This way," said Kalith. "It is safe."

Kalith guided them into the building and through a gateway into a small, featureless room. The floor was dark brown earth, but three of the walls were solid metal and the fourth was a shimmering, glittering barrier of blue-white electricity. They were in a cell. The gateway popped softly as it closed behind them. Kalith hadn't followed them through.

Ambassador Kurtz stood on the opposite side of the electrical barrier. Two guards stood beside him, ominous clouds of dark-gray energy crackling with menace. Another gateway was set in the wall behind Kurtz, this one active. The gateway shimmered, and Kalith entered the room.

"What is the meaning of this?" said Doctor Zheng.

"You are murderers," said Kurtz. His voice was calm,

self-assured. "Will stand trial."

"For murdering who?" said Glitch. "What's going on?"

Kurtz regarded him for a moment. "Humans are attacking. Planet collapses. Many Invisitude dead."

"Humans?" said Glitch. He looked at Anderson, his faced filled with confusion.

Doctor Zheng raised her hands to her head. "No! That can't be true. Why would Earth attack this planet?"

Kurtz snorted. "History shows pattern. Humans destroy humans. Humans destroy planet. Now destroy Invisitude."

"How do you know Earth is responsible for the attack?" said Glitch.

"Saboteur in city. Destroys buildings. Kills Invisitude."

"I don't believe it," said Doctor Zheng.

"It is true," said Kalith. "I have seen."

Doctor Zheng shook her head.

"It's Smith," said Glitch. "He has to be the one doing this."

"Glitch is right," said Anderson. "Smith is acting on his own. He has his own motives."

Kurtz stormed toward the cell, flashes of red cascading across his body. "Cannot believe. Will not believe. History reveals truth."

Doctor Zheng turned toward Kalith, pleading with her. "Please, Kalith. You have to believe us when we say we know nothing about this."

Kalith looked at Zheng. She lowered her head. "I cannot know."

"What are you going to do?" said Glitch.

Kurtz had recovered control of his emotions. He stepped back from the cell. "Defend ourselves."

Kalith turned to Kurtz. "No. You cannot. That is unnecessary."

"It is necessary."

Kurtz swept across the room, stopping inches from Kalith, and they stood facing each other, a myriad of colors flickering through their bodies. Tendrils of energy formed around them, waving and shuddering as though they were being battered by the wind.

Kurtz's body turned scarlet, flooding with rage. Kalith moved backward slightly, clouds of blood-red energy bursting across her body. Kurtz grew taller, raising himself up until he stood at least a foot above Kalith. The clusters of red in Kalith's body faded. One by one, the patches of red vanished, turning to yellow, then blue. Kurtz turned away in a blaze of scarlet and left the room.

"What happened, Kalith?" said Doctor Zheng.

Kalith didn't respond. She just stood, staring at the space where Kurtz had been standing as though she was waiting for him to return. Eventually, she looked up. "I am sorry."

"What's he going to do?" said Anderson.

Glitch swallowed. The tension in Anderson's voice was making him nervous.

"Attack Earth."

"No!" said Doctor Zheng. "We have to stop him. You have to let us out."

Kalith shook her head slowly. "I am sorry. Cannot do that."

"She doesn't trust us," said Glitch. "She thinks we're involved somehow."

Doctor Zheng moved forward until she was almost touching the energy field. "Please, Kalith. You have to believe us when we say we would never do anything like this. Earth has nothing to gain by attacking you. This is the work of one man… a madman, a terrorist. We are not like that."

A scattering of red flashed through Kalith's body. "History suggests otherwise."

"She's got a point," said Glitch.

The doctor glared at him. "I admit there have been times when the human race has made bad decisions, but this is different. This is our first contact with an intelligent race. Proof that we're not alone in the universe. Mankind has spent decades trying to prove the existence of extraterrestrial life. Why would we throw that all away by launching an unprovoked attack?"

"She has a point, too," said Glitch.

"Glitch…" hissed Anderson.

He mouthed an apology at her.

Kalith considered the doctor's words. The blue energy that made up her body grew more intense, thickening and glowing brighter. Seconds dragged by. There was a rumble, like thunder, and the ground shuddered. For a moment, it looked as though Kalith would relent, then she turned and walked out of the room. The guards followed her out, leaving them alone in the cell.

Glitch rubbed his hands down his face. "What now, Captain?"

"I don't know." Anderson crouched and picked up a small pebble from the ground. Waving Glitch and the doctor away from the energy field, she threw the stone.

Glitch tensed, expecting an explosion or an electrostatic crackle, or at least a shower of sparks. All that happened was the pebble bounced off the energy field as though it had hit a brick wall. It landed on the ground and rolled to a stop.

"Well," said Glitch, "that was pretty uneventful."

There was another muffled explosion somewhere off in the distance, and the ground shook again.

"How is Smith doing this?" said Glitch. "How is he destroying an entire planet?"

"It doesn't matter how he's doing it," said Anderson. "He is, and we need to stop Kurtz before the attack on Earth. Any ideas, Doctor?"

The doctor walked over to the gateway in the cell and ran her fingers over the raised controls, pressing and twisting them.

"That doesn't work," said Glitch.

"Feel free to come up with a better idea, Dwayne," said the doctor, her voice hard.

"I'm sorry, Doctor Zheng, but I left my portable teleportation device back on the *U.S.S. We're Screwed*."

Anderson rolled her eyes and held out her hands, palms facing the two of them. "Will you two children cut it out?

That isn't helping."

Glitch flinched and looked at his feet, blushing. Doctor Zheng looked as though she was about to say something but didn't. Anderson stared at them, daring them to speak. When they didn't, she crouched and examined the ground where the energy field met the floor. There was a loud buzz, and the energy field dissipated.

"Let's go," said Glitch, and he stepped forward.

Anderson grabbed his shoulder, pulling him back. "Hold on."

She picked up a few pebbles and scattered them in front of her. They landed safely on the other side of the barrier.

Kalith glided into the room through the gateway. "It is disabled."

"What happened?" said Glitch. "You changed your mind?"

"Yes. Doctor speaks truthfully. Decided to trust. You must go. Very little time."

"Go where?" asked Glitch.

"Home."

Glitch held up his hands. "You want us to go home right before Kurtz attacks? I'd rather take my chances here. Those So-lang seemed pretty cool."

"No. You must leave. Must warn them. Prepare for inevitable."

The doctor shook her head. "We can't go home. We have to stop Kurtz."

"Impossible. Weapon launches soon."

"Weapon?" said Glitch.

"Asteroid launcher."

"An asteroid gun? Holy…"

"Kalith," said the doctor, "we can't leave while there's still a chance we can stop the attack on Earth."

Kalith looked at them. A river of pale blue ran from her head, where the brain would be on a human, and down to her chest, where it fanned out in all directions. The threads of blue pulsed softly a few times before fading to nothing. She sighed, reached over to the gateway, and adjusted the controls. The silver surface of the gateway shimmered, a series of concentric waves rippling across its surface for a few seconds.

"Destination has changed."

Anderson looked uncertain. "Where will it take us?"

"To weapon controls."

Glitch was doubtful. Kalith might have just faked changing the destination. If they ended up back on Earth, she could close the gateway, and there would be nothing any of them could do. "How do we know that?"

Without speaking, Kalith moved through the gateway.

Glitch looked at Anderson, eyebrows raised. "Maybe she just fancied a trip to Earth."

"Only one way to find out," said Anderson, and she followed Kalith through the gateway.

Doctor Zheng looked at Glitch.

He bowed with a broad sweep of his arm. "After you, Doctor."

The doctor rolled her eyes and stepped through the

gateway. Smiling, Glitch followed her.

They came out into a long, wide corridor lit by a series of white strips embedded in the ceiling. It was empty, but there was a doorway twenty feet away. Shadows flickered across the wall opposite it, cast by something beyond the opening.

Glitch checked the corridor for Invisitude. "Anyone got a plan?"

"Working on it," said Anderson. "Kalith, what's in that room?"

"Launch controls. Targeting equipment."

"And... Invisitude?"

"Two guards. Ambassador Kurtz."

"How long do we have?"

"A short time."

Anderson let out a slow breath. Glitch looked at her puffed-out cheeks, her lips. He turned away when she realized he was staring at her.

"Okay," said Anderson. "Kalith and I will go in first and try to distract them. Doctor, Glitch, you follow five seconds later. Look for the control panel and find a way to stop the launch. Kalith, do you have any weapons?"

"I can disrupt. Perhaps slow guards. Not for long."

"Give us as much time as you can. We'll go on three. Everyone ready?"

Glitch and the doctor nodded. Kalith seemed less sure, but after a brief hesitation, she nodded, too.

"One... two... three!"

Kalith darted down the corridor with Anderson close

behind. Glitch counted to five, then he and Zheng followed. Someone shouted from inside the room. A crackle of electricity was followed by a pained scream. Energy filled the air, and the hairs on the back of Glitch's hands stood up as he turned the corner.

The control room was dominated by a display screen that ran the length of one wall. It showed an intricate tower built from dozens of metal bars or pipes, an inverted cone made from scaffolding. It had been built out in the desert somewhere, and it was huge—the handful of trees and buildings scattered around its base were tiny in comparison.

A control panel covered in dozens of silver plates and several small displays showing multiple views of the cone structure dominated the wall opposite the display. Ambassador Kurtz stood next to it with a guard, a seething mass of gray and red energy. Anderson was lying on the ground, clutching her left shoulder.

Kalith was nearby, standing between Anderson and another guard. The two watched each other warily, not moving. Glitch smelled ozone in the air.

Kurtz saw Glitch and the doctor and pointed at them. "Stop them."

They split up, the doctor heading right and Glitch left. Kurtz's guard hesitated then started in Glitch's direction. A long tendril of energy snaked toward Glitch, crackling and sparking. Glitch dodged right, and the line of energy flew past him, snapping into the wall like a whip.

There was a bang, painfully loud inside the enclosed

space, and a wave of hot air washed over Glitch. A second tendril of energy flew toward him. He twisted sideways, but it was too late. The energy hit Glitch's chest, and he screamed. The impact sent him slamming into the wall. Glitch's legs buckled, and he slumped to the ground. Blackness seeped into the edges of his vision as the guard advanced toward him.

On the other side of the room, Doctor Zheng had reached Kurtz. She stood in front of him, eyeing the control panel warily.

Anderson had pushed herself backward, away from Kalith and the guard, and she was trying to stand. Her legs shook, refusing to cooperate. There was a black scorch mark on her left shoulder, and thin wisps of smoke drifted from the burned fabric of her jacket. She slumped back down to the floor.

The guard loomed over Glitch. Glitch's heart was pounding, and his chest was on fire. He felt the charred remains of his T-shirt sticking to his flesh and smelled the sickly-sweet smell of burnt skin. Glitch shifted his position, and fresh waves of pain flooded his body. Passing out seemed like a very good idea.

Doctor Zheng made another attempt at reasoning with Kurtz. "Earth is not attacking the Invisitude. These are the actions of one man. We can help you find him and stop him."

"Lies," said Kurtz. Behind him, a row of lights turned green, and there was a brief high-pitched beep. He reached toward the controls. Energy leapt from his fingers and danced across the panel, flickering between the metal plates. When he pulled his hands away, he gestured toward the wall display. "Watch."

On the screen, bright white arcs of energy leapt across the metal scaffolding, fingers of lightning climbing up from the base of the structure. They spread outward, jumping from point to point. Clouds of dust swirled around the structure, obscuring its base.

His injuries momentarily forgotten, Glitch stared at the screen. Whatever he thought of the Invisitude, they knew how to put on a light show.

A series of searing blue flashes appeared, scattered through the center of the cone. They pulsed and flickered, leaving bright spots on Glitch's vision.

Then the fingers of energy around the structure's base contracted. They rushed inward, creating a sea of bright white light that swept upward. The image shook, and something dark and huge flew up the center of the tower. As it vanished out of sight, the white light dissipated. Within seconds, all that remained was a swirling mass of dust drifting away from the base of the tower.

Doctor Zheng stepped toward Kurtz. "What have you done?"

Glitch half expected Kurtz to reply with, "You started it," but he didn't. He didn't say anything.

Anderson pushed herself to her feet and staggered toward the doctor. Zheng put her arm under Anderson's shoulder, and Glitch saw the captain sag a little.

Kurtz moved across the room. Streaks of red flickered

across his body, then he motioned to the guards and left. The guards moved toward the humans, long ribbons of energy snaking through the air around them.

CHAPTER TWENTY
One Last Hope

Glitch, Captain Anderson, and Doctor Zheng arrive in the Invisitude city. Most of the buildings have been damaged or destroyed, and fires rage all around. The Invisitude, Kalith, guides them through a gateway, and they find themselves in a cell. Ambassador Kurtz informs them that the Invisitude are under attack by the human race, and the Invisitude intend to retaliate by launching an asteroid at Earth. Kalith relents and frees the humans, and they go to the weapon control center to try to stop Kurtz. Kurtz's guards overwhelm them, and the asteroid is launched.

"What have you done?" said Doctor Zheng.

Glitch half expected Kurtz to reply with, "You started it," but he didn't say anything at all.

Wincing from her injuries, Anderson pushed herself to her feet and took a few unsteady steps toward the doctor. The doctor slipped her arm under Anderson's shoulder, and the captain sagged a little.

Kurtz moved across the room to the doorway. He stood there, looking back into the room for a moment, then gestured to the guards and left. The guards moved toward the humans. Long ribbons of dark energy snaked through the air around them.

Glitch laughed. It started as a high-pitched chuckle but quickly evolved into full-bodied, shoulder-shuddering laughter. "Yes, you did. You invaded Poland," he said, somehow managing to find space between fits of giggles to speak.

Every laugh, every guffaw sent fresh waves of pain burning through his body. Glitch clutched at his sides, trying to still the laughter long enough to drag in enough oxygen to remain conscious.

If some part of Glitch's mind was expecting the sudden outburst of hilarity to distract the guards, it didn't work. The guard standing over Glitch didn't respond.

Anderson looked at Kalith, but Kalith didn't acknowledge her.

The smell of ozone filled the air. Glitch looked up, and the laughter died on his lips as the guard towering over him flashed red. Raw energy crackled through its body. Glitch's veins were filled with ice water, and he wondered if his life would flash before his eyes as he died. That would be a depressing experience.

The guard swept its arms forward.

Glitch rolled sideways as two bolts of energy slammed into the ground where he'd been lying. His chest screamed in pain as he forced himself to his feet and threw himself across the room.

There was an explosion of blue-white light. Something hit Glitch, and he was thrown across the room again. He hit the wall, bounced off, and collapsed to the floor. Glitch closed his eyes. His back hurt, his chest hurt, his head hurt. He was so tired; maybe he could just go to sleep.

Red and blue light flashed through his eyelids. A static hiss assaulted his ears. He swung his hands around, trying to find the volume control or an on/off switch. A wave of heat washed over him, bringing with it the smell of burning metal. Blackness rose up around Glitch, and he lay back in its comforting embrace.

Something pressed against Glitch's shoulder, a hand shaking him awake. He groaned and reached for his blanket. Fire wrapped around his chest, snapping him awake.

Anderson's face peered down at him, a sheen of sweat across her forehead. She smiled. "I thought you were dead."

Glitch coughed, the movement igniting fresh pain in his chest. "You know me. A regular Snake Plissken." Fear gripped Glitch by the back of his neck. "What about the guards?"

"It's okay. Kalith took care of them."

Glitch leaned past Anderson. Kalith was standing at the door to the control room, looking out into the corridor.

She looked back at Glitch. "You are awake. We must go. Return to Earth."

Glitch squeezed his eyes shut. He knew that was a bad idea; he just couldn't remember why. When he opened his eyes again, he was looking at the desert scene on the giant video screen. "What about the asteroid?"

Kalith seemed to grow smaller. "I am sorry."

"But it didn't look that big," said Glitch. "Maybe it won't do much damage."

"Energy charges fitted," said Kalith, shaking her head. "To create explosion."

Glitch felt the blood rush from his face. "We need to stop the asteroid before it gets to Earth."

"Too late. On collision course."

"There must be a way to stop it," said Zheng.

"No. I am sorry."

"What about the explosives? Can we trigger them from here?" asked Anderson.

"No. Is no solution."

Glitch ran his fingers through his hair. "What if we were on the asteroid?"

For a moment, Kalith didn't respond. Eventually, she said, "Yes."

"So all we need to do is get to the asteroid and detonate the explosives before it reaches Earth. That way everyone gets to experience a nice fireworks display rather than a new ice age or whatever."

"There's only one problem with that, Dwayne," said Doctor Zheng. "How do we get to the asteroid?"

Glitch dragged in a breath, wincing at the pain. "Kalith, we saw some sort of vehicle out in the desert. It looked like a shuttle or an aircraft of some sort."

"Shuttle. Transports… supplies."

"Are there any in the city?"

"Yes."

Glitch winced again as a stabbing pain tore into his shoulder. The world around him blurred. "Could we use one to get to the asteroid?"

Kalith didn't respond.

"Kalith?" said Zheng.

"Yes. Shuttle is capable."

Glitch let his head fall back against the wall. "Problem solved."

"What do you think, Kalith?" said Anderson. "Could it work?"

"Perhaps. But very dangerous. Survival unlikely."

Glitch moaned. The burning in his chest was growing stronger every second, and his right arm was going numb. There was a thick metallic taste in his mouth, and every now and again, the world around him blurred, spinning out of focus for a few seconds. He was convinced his skin would flake away if he moved too much. At least he wouldn't have to wait for the poison to kill him.

Kalith leaned over Glitch. "Do not move."

Glitch closed his eyes. Hundreds of tiny pinpricks of energy danced across his chest, leaving behind a soothing, cool numbness that spread through his body. The air around him was filled with the smell of something a lot like burned toast. He felt a gentle pressure centered on his heart. Energy spread out from his chest, chasing away the numbness. Glitch's right hand twitched, the muscles reacting to the energy coursing through them.

He felt the pressure lift from his skin, leaving behind a cool, tingling sensation that was not entirely pleasant. His chest was tight, bruised, and he found it hard to breathe. At least he didn't feel like a cannibal's dinner anymore, although he was sure he could still smell the subtle aroma of long pig.

Glitch spent a couple of minutes getting to his feet. When he plucked up the courage to look down at his chest, he was surprised to find that he was mostly intact. His skin was red and raw, and there were several scarlet welts a few centimeters long, but he'd been expecting to see imploded ribs and dangling internal organs. His chest still felt tight, but his breathing was becoming easier. He lightly brushed his fingers over the welts. They hurt, but the pain was bearable. He figured he owed Kalith his life.

"Thank you, Kalith."

"No thanks required."

Glitch looked at Anderson. "Right, let's go and save the world."

Anderson raised a hand. "No, Glitch. You should stay here."

"And do what, exactly? Hide in the caves living off moss until Kurtz or one of his goons finds me? I'd rather take my chances in the shuttle." Anderson started to protest, but Glitch cut her off. "There's not even any

Netflix here."

"Much as it pains me to say this," said the doctor, "he's right. We can't leave him here."

"Thank you."

Anderson tipped back her head and sighed at the ceiling. "Okay."

"Kalith," said Glitch, "can you take us to one of the shuttles?"

Kalith bowed slightly. "Please follow."

"Kalith," said Anderson, "whatever happens, make sure you stop that asteroid."

Kalith hesitated for a moment before nodding. She led them out of the room and through a gateway that brought them to an alley between two low-slung buildings. Like the rest of the city, the walls were metal, but they were built from slatted sheets, like large louvered windows. The buildings were undamaged. A fine haze of smoke hung in the air, and every now and again, the ground shook or the sound of a distant explosion reached them.

"Shuttle that way," said Kalith, gesturing to Glitch's right.

They walked down the alley and out onto the open expanse of a landing zone. There were five pads. Two stood empty, but the other three held shuttles like the one they'd seen crash-landed in the desert. Even intact, the shuttles seemed boxy and simplistic, a halfhearted slope on the front the only concession to aerodynamics. They didn't look as though they'd fly.

The landing pads were surrounded by six more of the

squat, louver-walled buildings. Beyond them lay the city. Fires raged across it, sending thick pillars of black smoke into the sky. With a flash of blue, one of the geogrid buildings collapsed, a twisted, burning tangle of metal.

Halfway across the landing area, pain hit Glitch again. Red-hot knives pierced his stomach, draining the strength from his legs. He stumbled forward.

Anderson caught him. "The poison?"

Glitch nodded and reached for the pouch containing the moss. Another burst of pain ripped through his body. The world around him turned gray. He fumbled with the pouch, battling the urge to just let the poison take him. But he managed to get hold of the moss, and he pushed it into his mouth and forced himself to swallow.

"Come on," said Anderson. "Let's get inside."

They'd almost reached the nearest shuttle when there was the sharp crack of gunfire. Bullets ricocheted off the ground in front of them, sending up plumes of dust. They ran, the bouncing movement sending angry razor blades ripping through Glitch's stomach. There was a deep rumbling sound, and the ground shifted. A jagged split opened up in the surface of the landing zone with a loud crack.

Kalith reached the shuttle first and ran a hand over a panel in its side. Servos hummed, and a metal doorway slid open, revealing the vehicle's interior. Inside, bright white lights flickered to life. Anderson pushed Glitch toward the door. A spray of bullets hit the side of the shuttle as Glitch threw himself inside.

There was more gunfire, and Anderson let out a cry. Glitch ducked his head around the door. Anderson was lying on the ground, clutching her leg. Blood oozed between her fingers and her face was contorted in pain, but at least she was alive. Doctor Zheng stood a few feet away from the shuttle, her hands raised.

A voice echoed across the landing zone. "So we meet again, Mr. Glitch."

Glitch's heart sank. It was Smith, but Glitch couldn't see where he was. There were plenty of buildings for him to hide in, and there was no way for Anderson or Doctor Zheng to get into the shuttle without being shot.

"It must be fate," shouted Glitch.

John Smith appeared around the corner of one of the buildings. He was carrying a bulky silver object that looked a lot like a pistol. The barrel was trained on Doctor Zheng.

Glitch glanced around the shuttle. The overall design was identical to the one they'd sheltered in, but there were no cages, and the cloth webbing that hung from the walls was intact. He saw no sign of Kalith, but the door leading to the front of the shuttle was closed. A rack stood nearby. It held three silver objects—pistols similar to the one Smith was carrying but a bit larger.

Glitch pulled one of the pistols free. The grip was big, with ridges in all the wrong places, but despite its bulk, the weapon was impossibly light. A series of unmarked buttons and dials sat above the weapon's grip. Glitch stared at them, trying to guess which might set the weapon to "stun." The gun wavered in his hands. The pain in his stomach had receded again, but his hands were shaking, and he felt woozy. Not the best time for a shootout. Glitch peered out the door. Smith's gun was still trained on Zheng.

"What now?" called Glitch. "You kill us?"

Smith pulled his head to the side to look at Glitch, a pained expression creasing his face. "Oh no, nothing as crude as that. I'm here in the name of justice, not vengeance. I want you to pay the price for your crimes."

"Our crimes?" said Zheng.

"Yes. Your completely unprovoked attack on this fair planet." He gestured toward the pillar of black smoke. "Your blatant disregard for the sanctity of Invisitude life."

Something moved beside one of the buildings, a flicker of steely gray. Ambassador Kurtz stepped onto the airfield, flanked by four of the red guards.

Servos whirred, and the door to the front of the shuttle opened. Kalith glided into the cargo hold. "Shuttle is ready. Must leave now."

"We're not leaving without them," said Glitch.

"Captain Anderson's instructions."

Glitch glared at Kalith. "We are *not* leaving without them."

Kalith didn't reply.

Glitch looked toward Smith. He hadn't seen the ambassador arrive.

"So," said Glitch, "you're setting us up?"

Smith shrugged. "I wouldn't put it quite like that. Oh,

all right. Yes, I'm setting you up. I hadn't really planned it this way, but when you showed up, everything just clicked into place."

"But why are you doing this? What do you want?"

"Oh, Dwayne." Smith stopped, correcting himself. "Sorry. Oh, Glitch. What does any man want? Power. When that asteroid hits the Earth, in about"—he mimed checking a watch—"an hour, it'll cause untold misery and chaos. The perfect time for me to return and lead the world into a brighter future."

"So let me get this straight. You've been triggering earthquakes, setting off explosions, and killing Invisitude all across the city to provoke an attack on Earth so that you can step in and take control of the planet?"

Smith waved the gun at Glitch with a broad grin. "Yes! Yes! That's it exactly. Such a clever boy."

"But how did you set off the earthquakes?"

"It's surprisingly easy, actually. The energy sources on this planet are remarkably powerful. Overload this, overload that, and before you know it, earthquakes! Destruction! Imminent collapse!"

"Did you hear that, Ambassador?" shouted Glitch. "This is the man who's been attacking the city. He's the one killing your people."

Smith swung round, pointing the gun at Ambassador Kurtz. "No. No!" His face contorted with anger. "Dammit! And I would have gotten away with it, too, if it hadn't been for you meddling kids!"

There was a pause as Glitch's brain caught up, then his

face flushed red. He was such an idiot.

Ambassador Kurtz and the guards glided across the landing zone and stood beside Smith.

Smith let the anger fade from his face, replacing it with a soulless smile. "Ambassador Kurtz, I'm glad you could make it. It seems I've tracked down the terrorists for you."

Ambassador Kurtz bowed toward Smith. "Thank you. We are grateful."

"I... I don't understand," said Glitch. "Why?"

"Their planet is dying," said Doctor Zheng. "They need Earth, but there aren't enough of them to take it by force. Smith is going to bring the Invisitude to Earth so that they can save the human race from the aftermath of the asteroid collision. Once they've done that, they'll be welcomed with open arms."

"Particularly when they're told that we were the ones who attacked the Invisitude," said Glitch.

"Ting!" said Smith. "We have a winner. Now, if you'd like to go with the ambassador, I can assure you your execution will be quite painful."

CHAPTER TWENTY-ONE
The Betrayal

Kalith stops Kurtz's guards from killing the humans. Kalith takes Glitch, Anderson, and Zheng to a shuttle which they hope they can use to destroy the asteroid hurtling toward Earth, but they are ambushed by John Smith, and Anderson is wounded. Ambassador Kurtz arrives, and Glitch, in an attempt to show that Smith is responsible for the attack on the Invisitude, manages to get Smith to reveal his plans.

"Did you hear that, Ambassador?" shouted Glitch. "This is the man who's been attacking the city. He's the one killing your people."

Smith swung round, pointing his gun at Ambassador Kurtz. "No. No!" His face contorted with anger. "Dammit! And I would have gotten away with it, too, if it hadn't been for you meddling kids!"

Glitch's face flushed red as Ambassador Kurtz glided silently across the landing zone to stand beside Smith.

Smith's anger faded away, replaced by a smile that

didn't reach his eyes. "Ambassador Kurtz, I'm glad you could make it. It seems I've tracked down the terrorists for you."

"Thank you. We are grateful."

"I… I don't understand," said Glitch. "Why?"

"Their planet is dying," said Doctor Zheng. "They need Earth, but there aren't enough of them to take it by force. Smith is going to bring the Invisitude to Earth so that they can save the human race from the aftermath of the asteroid collision. Once they've done that, they'll be welcomed with open arms."

"Particularly when they realize that we attacked the Invisitude," said Glitch.

"Ting!" said Smith. "We have a winner. Now, if you'd like to go with the ambassador, I can assure you your execution will be quite painful."

Glitch pulled himself back into the shuttle and looked at the gun in his hand, trying to make sense of the bewildering array of buttons and dials mounted along its length. He had no clue what any of them did.

"Crap." He swept his fingers along the side of the gun, randomly flicking and twisting the controls.

Then he leaned around the door, aimed at Smith, and squeezed the trigger. The gun hummed, vibrating with energy. Glitch braced himself for a *Dirty Harry* kickback, but it never came. The shot just seemed to materialize in front of the gun and hover there for a fraction of a second before racing toward its target with a high-pitched whistle and a streak of blue light that stung Glitch's eyes. The shot went wide, hitting one of the slatted buildings and erupting in a searing flash of blue-white light and flame and molten metal.

Smith ducked, firing wildly as he dodged sideways. Bullets bounced off the side of the shuttle. Glitch fired again. This time his shot fell short, and the ground a few feet away from Smith exploded. Backing away, Kurtz flashed red. The red guards advanced toward the shuttle.

Doctor Zheng was already running toward Anderson.

"Get in," screamed Glitch as he fired again. He aimed high to avoid hitting Zheng, and the shot flew across the landing zone, disappearing between two buildings. There was a muffled thump of an explosion. Glitch became aware of movement behind him—Kalith.

"We must leave."

"As soon as they're inside," shouted Glitch.

Zheng reached Anderson. She crouched beside the fallen captain, slung her arm beneath her shoulder, and helped Anderson to her feet. Anderson's pants were soaked with blood, and her face was pale.

A bullet whistled past Glitch and slammed into the back wall of the shuttle. Smith had positioned himself at the corner of one of the buildings, his back against the wall to provide some cover. He was still firing at them.

Glitch aimed at Smith and fired. The shot caught the corner of the building, right beside Smith. The wall exploded, scattering fragments of white-hot metal across the landing zone. Smith was thrown backward, and he slammed into the building opposite. He fell to the ground and lay in a crumpled, unmoving heap.

There was a high-pitched whine from somewhere behind Glitch. A cloud of dust rolled away from the rear of the shuttle, and the metal vibrated beneath his feet.

The red guards were almost at the shuttle, and Glitch fired at the nearest one. His aim was getting better, his years of videogames finally paying off. His shot hit the center of the guard. A spider's web of blue energy crackled across its body. There was a blinding flash of light and rush of static, and the guard was gone.

Glitch helped Anderson into the shuttle. Anderson's face twisted in pain as she dragged herself across the floor. Glitch fired off a couple more shots as Zheng threw herself on board. Not waiting to see whether he'd connected with his targets, he slammed his hand against the control panel next to the door. Unlike the rest of the Invisitude devices, this one had actual, physical buttons, and the door slid closed as the shuttle began to lift off.

As the doctor searched for something to use as a tourniquet, Glitch joined Kalith. The cockpit of the shuttle was dominated by a curved video display showing a one-hundred-eighty-degree view of the outside world. Beneath the screen were two identical control panels. Each panel had seven silver disks on it and a set of four small display screens showing various scenes outside the craft. Kalith was standing next to the right-hand panel. Tendrils of energy leapt from her hands and crackled across the control panel.

Glitch steadied himself as the shuttle leaned forward

and accelerated away from the landing pad. There was a muffled thump and the shuttle rocked, then they were flying over the city.

"Will they follow us?" said Glitch.

"Yes," said Kalith.

She shifted position, and another thread of energy snaked free of her form. When it touched the control panel, it scattered, sending a dozen blue children across the silver disks. One of the screens on the control panel flickered, and the video feed of the landing site was replaced by text. A dozen lines, symbols Glitch didn't recognize, scrolled up the side of the screen. The shuttle accelerated, leaning to the right.

The city raced beneath them, growing smaller and smaller as the shuttle climbed. They were rapidly approaching the protective bubble that surrounded the city. Kalith adjusted the controls again, and the display screen dimmed.

"Hold on," said Kalith.

Glitch barely had time to clutch the edge of the control panel before, with a thump, the shuttle lurched forward. The display screen washed out, glowing white. The sound of the shuttle's engines became muffled for a second, then Glitch's ears popped and the noise came back stronger than ever. The shuttle shuddered and rattled. It lurched downward, pitching Glitch to the right. Behind him, the doctor cursed. The whine of the engines increased to a scream that threatened to tear Glitch's teeth from his head.

There was another thump, and the shuttle stopped

shaking and leveled off. The sound of the engines returned to less ear-shattering levels, and the display screen faded to black. Kalith adjusted the controls, and the display flickered and resolved into a view of space. And Earth.

Anderson let out a cry, and Glitch moved back to check on her.

She was sitting on the floor, her back against the side of the shuttle. Her eyes were closed, and her face was pale and slick with sweat. Doctor Zheng had torn the leg off Anderson's pants and tied it around her thigh. The cloth was already deep scarlet, and a thin pool of blood was spreading across the floor beneath her leg. Zheng had her hands pressed against the wound.

"How is she?" said Glitch.

"She's alive, and the bleeding is slowing, but she's lost a lot of blood, and her pulse is weak."

"I'm not dead yet," said Anderson in a high voice.

Glitch tried to smile but couldn't. "Kalith, Scarlett is hurt. Can you help her?"

Kalith joined them at the back of the shuttle. She knelt beside Anderson and reached toward her injured leg. "This will hurt."

Doctor Zheng grabbed the captain's hand. Anderson screamed as electricity leapt from Kalith's hands and wrapped around her leg. Thin wisps of smoke drifted up from the wound, and the smell of burnt flesh filled the air. The electricity retreated.

Kalith removed her hands and examined the wound. "Keep her still." She returned to the front of the shuttle.

Anderson's screams faded away, and she leaned back against the wall. Doctor Zheng pressed her fingers against Anderson's neck, checking her pulse. Zheng's face was full of concern, and when she pulled her hand away, she seemed only slightly happier.

"Scarlett, can you hear me?"

Anderson's eyelids fluttered open, then she moaned and closed them again. She mumbled something.

"Okay, get some rest," said Doctor Zheng.

Anderson frowned. "The asteroid…"

Glitch looked at the screen. If there was an asteroid out there, he couldn't see it.

"We are tracking," said Kalith.

"How long until we get there?" said Glitch.

"Four Earth minutes."

"What happened to Smith and Kurtz?" said Zheng.

"Smith is dead. I don't know about Kurtz," said Glitch. "He ran."

On the display, a red bolt of energy flashed past the front of the shuttle. Kalith's hands flew to the controls, electricity flashing from her fingertips. "They are pursuing."

Kalith swept her hands across the controls again. A high-pitched whistle came from somewhere above the shuttle as Kalith returned fire—a super-sized version of the noise made by the pistol Glitch had used. There was an explosion, and sparks burst from the wall. The ship juddered and dipped.

Kalith fired again, and the shuttle tilted to the left.

Another shuttle, identical to theirs, rushed past them. Kalith turned the ship back to the right and fired again. The first shot went wide, disappearing over the shuttle. The second caught the back corner, near the engine. There was a burst of light as the engine exploded. The enemy craft twisted, spinning sideways and leaving a trail of metal debris in its wake. Searing white light overwhelmed the display as the enemy shuttle was engulfed by another explosion. Kalith pushed the shuttle downward. Shards of metal bounced off the hull, and the shuttle was buffeted around as they passed beneath the disintegrating craft. Something clanged off the wall behind Glitch, and he flinched, waiting for the inevitable decompression to pull him out into the void. Then they were in clear space again.

Kalith leveled off the shuttle and called to the back of the ship. "Injuries?"

Glitch looked at Doctor Zheng and Anderson, and they shook their heads. "We're fine. That was some good shooting, Kalith."

"More may follow."

"How far to the asteroid?" said Glitch.

Kalith gestured toward the display screen. "It is visible."

Glitch made his way to the cabin and searched for the asteroid. It took him a few seconds to find it. It was unexpectedly smooth, more like a large gray bullet than an asteroid from the movies. Kalith adjusted the heading of the shuttle, directing it straight toward the asteroid.

The asteroid was rotating along its central axis, adding

to the image of a giant bullet made of rock hurtling toward Earth. Glitch wondered if NASA had spotted it yet, whether presidents and prime ministers were being woken in the middle of the night and hurried to the underground bunkers where the great and the good went to hide during times of emergency.

Kalith adjusted the controls. Servos whined again as the guns targeted the asteroid. "Weapon is ready."

Kalith seemed to be waiting for Glitch to give her the okay to fire, and Glitch felt the warm thrill of excitement. Ever since he was a kid, he'd wanted to command a spaceship. Now he was with an alien being, saving Earth. He was preparing to give the command when Kalith fired the guns.

Four parcels of energy flew from the shuttle and traced a line along the length of the asteroid. They seemed too small as they were swallowed up by the gray bulk of the rock, but clusters of bright red light flared across the asteroid where they hit. The red light spread across the rock's surface, leaping from point to point until it was covered in a web of red fire.

Then the asteroid tore itself apart, sending thousands of fragments spinning into space. Rock pounded the shuttle, the sound reverberating off the metal walls. Glitch yelled as a lump of asteroid the size of a small car spun toward them, filling the display screen.

Kalith swept her hand across the controls and twisted the shuttle sideways. There was a heavy thump, and the vehicle shuddered violently. A panel on the wall exploded in a shower of sparks, and the lights flickered and went out. An alarm pulsed.

Emergency lighting kicked in, bathing the shuttle in a red glow. More pieces of the asteroid hit the ship, and another panel exploded. Red lights lit up across the control panels, and another alarm, high pitched and rapid, joined the first. The shuttle twisted sideways as Kalith fought to maintain control. The shuttle righted itself and accelerated into clear space. Kalith silenced the alarms.

Glitch spun a full three hundred sixty degrees, looking for damage. Apart from a few panels that were still sparking and the fine mist of smoke hanging in the air, the shuttle seemed intact. Zheng and Anderson were still sitting on the floor. The captain had closed her eyes again.

"Is she okay?" said Glitch.

"Yes, she is," said Anderson, opening her eyes again. "But she would really like to go home now."

Glitch nodded his agreement and turned back to the display screen. The view of space had been replaced by a larger version of the text display Glitch had seen on the control panel earlier. Kalith hurriedly adjusted the shuttle's controls. The whine from the shuttle's engines grew louder, steadily increasing in pitch.

"Kalith, what's wrong?" said Glitch.

"Shuttle is damaged. Unable to control."

"But you can fix it, right?"

Kalith switched the display back to the view outside. Earth filled the screen. "No, I cannot."

CHAPTER TWENTY-TWO
Collision Course

Fleeing from John Smith and the Invisitude, Glitch provides cover while Doctor Zheng gets an injured Captain Anderson into the shuttle. Smith returns fire, but Glitch causes an explosion that sends Smith crashing into a wall, killing him. With the humans aboard, Kalith launches the shuttle, and they chase the asteroid hurtling toward Earth. After fighting off their pursuers, Kalith destroys the asteroid, but despite her best efforts, debris from the explosion hits the shuttle.

Kalith stood in front of the shuttle's control panel. Her hands darted to and fro as she made adjustments. The whine of the engines grew louder, steadily increasing in pitch.

"Kalith, what's wrong?" said Glitch.

Kalith switched the one-hundred-eighty-degree display at the front of the shuttle back to the view outside. Earth filled the screen. "Shuttle is damaged. Unable to control."

"But you can fix it, right?"

Kalith moved across the cabin to the damaged wall panel. Wires dangled from the tear in the wall. "No, I cannot."

With a loud bang, sparks burst from the damaged panel. Earth loomed large on the video display.

"But this ship is built to withstand a reentry, isn't it?"

"Ship is," said Kalith. "You are not."

"What's that supposed to mean?"

Anderson appeared at the door to the cabin, Zheng supporting her. "She means there's no heat shielding. Or at least not enough to protect us."

"Captain is correct."

Glitch wiped sweat from his brow; real or imagined, he was suddenly very warm. "So basically we're going to be cooked alive?"

"Basically, yes," said Anderson.

"Kalith, will the heat harm you?" asked Zheng.

"No. I can dissipate."

The doctor looked almost relieved. Glitch got the impression she was more concerned about Kalith's survival than her own.

"Can we use that?" he asked. "Can you dissipate the heat for us?"

As Kalith considered the question, Glitch pressed his hand against the wall of the shuttle. It felt warm, he was sure of it.

Anderson saw the look on Glitch's face. "Don't worry. We're not close enough yet. Even at this speed, we've got some time."

Glitch nodded, hoping she was right but not convinced.

"Perhaps," said Kalith. "Encase shuttle. May protect you. A small chance. Cannot be sure."

A smile broke over Glitch's face. "So let's do that."

Kalith shook her head. "Does not help. Trajectory incorrect. Cannot adjust. Shuttle will destruct."

Glitch felt his last shreds of hope evaporate. "There must be something we can do?" He winced at the fear in his voice.

Kalith gestured toward the damaged panel. "Controls are damaged."

Glitch went to the panel and picked through the wires. They were color coded. Despite the damage, most of the wires were intact, and those that weren't could easily be repaired. A flash of hope flared inside Glitch. "I can probably fix this."

That hope died again when Glitch pulled the wires to one side and peered inside the panel. The wires led to a circuit board, roughly four inches across. Glitch didn't recognize the components, but it was clear from the scorch marks and the blackened, melted clumps of metal that reattaching a few wires wouldn't solve anything. "Or maybe not."

Glitch reached into the opening and pulled at the circuit board. It twisted a little then popped free. Glitch pulled out the board, scraping his knuckles on the edge of the opening in the process. The damaged wires were clipped onto the circuit board. Glitch removed them then flipped the board over. There was a connector on the back and a matching slot inside the control panel.

The shuttle shuddered, the hull groaning. Glitch glanced at the video screen. Earth filled it completely now. Anderson and Zheng were watching him expectantly while Kalith continued to adjust the shuttle's controls.

"Kalith," said Glitch, "does this shuttle carry any spare parts?"

Kalith pointed toward a panel marked with a yellow triangle in the wall at the back of the cabin. "Perhaps there."

It took a few seconds for Glitch to work out how to open the panel. In the end, he found the combination of pressing and twisting that unlatched it, and the panel swung open. Inside was a metal cube with a handle on top, like a toolbox. He pulled it out, opened the catches on each side, and silently uttering a quick prayer, removed the lid.

The box was lined with a dense, foam-like material that had a series of slots cut into it. Six of the slots held circuit boards of various sizes and designs. Two slots were empty. Glitch ran his fingers over the edges of the circuit board, but he could already see one of the empty slots was the right size for the damaged board. None of the others matched it.

"Dammit!" Glitch threw the broken board across the cabin, and it careened off the wall, breaking apart and scattering pieces across the floor. He looked up at Anderson and Zheng. "Sorry."

Anderson nodded. The shuttle lurched, bouncing her against the cabin wall, and she winced. Blood oozed from the wound in her leg again, and her skin was pale and waxy.

Glitch was about to tell Anderson to sit down when another yellow triangle caught his eye. There was another panel like the one he'd just opened on the opposite side of the cabin. He almost threw himself across the floor to it, his sudden movement eliciting a yelp of surprise from Zheng.

He popped open the panel, his heart thundering as he yanked out another cube. His hands shook as he flicked open the catches. This time, he didn't bother with a prayer; he just pulled the lid off and threw it away.

Again, two of the slots in the foam were empty. For a moment, Glitch thought the same two circuit boards were missing. Then he realized the box was the opposite way round. The matching board was still there. He slipped the board out of the box, just managing to contain his desperation enough to take care not to damage it.

As Glitch moved back to the control panel, he checked the circuit board. It looked intact, and the connector on the back matched. Spreading apart the damaged wiring, he pushed the board into position. The connector snapped easily into place.

"How long do we have left?" he asked.

There was a pause, then Kalith replied. "Nine Earth minutes."

Glitch let out a slow breath, trying to calm his nerves.

The ends of the wires were labeled with a complex series of symbols, and there were matching marks on the circuit board, but they were small and hard to read.

He started with the undamaged wires first, double and triple checking the symbols on each one before carefully snapping them into place on the circuit board. The connectors were keyed, so he couldn't get them the wrong way around, but still, Glitch wasn't completely convinced he was getting them all right. Twice he had to switch the position of almost identically marked cables when he realized he'd gotten them wrong.

When he was as confident as he could be that he'd reattached the intact cables correctly, he switched his attention to the ones that had been torn apart. At least there were only four of them.

The first two were easy enough to fix. One was blue, the other an orange-red, and Glitch simply stripped the ends of each wire and twisted them together. The last two weren't quite so simple. The colors were very similar, and the wires were badly damaged. Even once Glitch had managed to twist them together, he couldn't be sure they'd hold.

Glitch pushed the last of the cables into the connector on the board and stepped back. "Okay, I think that's it. Kalith, are the controls back?"

It felt like an age before Kalith replied. "No."

Glitch pressed the heels of his hands against his forehead, frustration welling inside him. The shuttle began to shake.

"It's okay," said Anderson. "Check the connections."

Glitch nodded and peered into the open panel. The symbols on the board swam, blurring together into a meaningless sea of chicken scratch. He squeezed his eyes shut, trying to block out the rattling of the shuttle. A hand touched his shoulder. It was Anderson.

Glitch checked the board again, working steadily across the connections, checking each one. He was almost on the last connection when he spotted the problem. Or *a* problem, anyway. Two of the damaged wires were touching, the exposed twists touching each other. Cursing, he pulled them apart. If he'd shorted out the circuit, they were screwed.

"Controls are working," said Kalith.

Glitch grinned. "Then get us out of here."

The shuttle bucked hard, skewing to the right and sending Glitch staggering across the cabin.

Kalith adjusted the controls. "Reduced power. Limited options. Entering Earth atmosphere."

Now Glitch really could feel the heat in the cabin. He pressed his hand against the shuttle wall. It was warm, and the look on Anderson's face told him that this time, he wasn't imagining it.

"Now would be a really good time to start shielding us," he said.

Kalith didn't respond. She just kept moving her hands over the shuttle's controls.

There was a loud crack from the back of the shuttle, and it rocked forward. Glitch heard Anderson cry out.

"Doctor, get the captain into the back and sit down. This could get bumpy."

Anderson started to protest, but the doctor cut her off. "There's nothing you can do, Scarlett."

Glitch joined Kalith at the front of the shuttle. "Let me guess, it's not working."

"It is working. Requires constant adjustment."

"So... you can't leave the controls to shield us?"

"You are correct."

Glitch looked at the controls. They meant nothing to him—just seven metal disks laid out in a seemingly random pattern. "Can I operate these?"

"Unknown."

"But I could try? If you showed me what to do?"

"Yes. But results uncertain."

"I've played a lot of video games."

"Do not underst—"

"Never mind. What do I need to do?"

Kalith placed her fingertips against three of the silver disks, and the image of Earth was replaced by a green vertical bar surrounded by a scrolling display of symbols similar to those on the circuit board. The green bar grew longer and turned an angry shade of red. Kalith shifted the position of her hand. It shrank and turned green again.

She pulled her hand away from the controls. "Place hand here."

It was awkward, but Glitch managed to contort his fingers so that he was touching the same disks Kalith had been. Sweat dripped from the end of his nose, and he was suddenly glad the screen no longer showed the approaching planet. "Now what?"

"Maintain green bar."

As Kalith spoke, the bar shrunk slightly and flickered red.

Glitch pressed against the metal disks, but they didn't move, and the bar stayed resolutely red. "But how?"

Kalith paused. "Cannot explain. Envisage correct result."

Glitch groaned inside. He'd never been much for hippy-dippy visualization techniques—he was too easily distracted. He tried pressing the disks again, this time picturing the bar turning green. The bar shrank again and stayed red.

"Too low. Raise shuttle front."

Glitch took a deep breath and focused his eyes on a scratch at the bottom of the display screen. He pictured the shuttle hurtling toward Earth, the hull glowing, a cone of orange flowing off the shuttle's blocky nose as it broke into the atmosphere. Around him, the shuttle rattled and shook. He added that to his mental image, letting his imaginary shuttle buck and rock. Then he imagined the shuttle's nose tipping back slightly.

"Good," said Kalith, snapping Glitch's focus back to the display.

The red bar grew again, turned green, then overshot and changed to red.

"Maintain green."

Glitch nodded. He wiped away a trickle of sweat that

was heading toward his eye. The heat was growing stronger by the second, and he was starting to feel lightheaded.

He let the picture of the shuttle reform in his mind. He tipped the nose forward again. Glitch found it hard to picture the shuttle and watch the bar, like patting your head and rubbing your stomach at the same time. He shifted his focus back to the screen. The bar wavered slightly then shrank and went green.

"Continue," said Kalith. She moved behind Glitch, out of sight.

A wall of blue energy wrapped across the display screen. It rippled and shifted for a moment, then was gone.

He couldn't be sure whether it was his imagination or not, but Glitch thought the temperature in the cabin dropped noticeably. The bar on the display snapped to its full length and turned red. A high-pitched pinging filled the air. Glitch pressed his fingers against the control panel and tried to picture the shuttle leaning forward. What he wouldn't do for a straightforward Xbox controller right now.

But it was getting easier to visualize the shuttle, and he didn't need as much detail. As Glitch pictured the shuttle tipping forward, the red bar shrank again, and to his relief, the pinging stopped.

Glitch began to be able to anticipate the bar's movements, raising and lowering the shuttle's nose before the bar turned red rather than after. Glitch let himself smile. The hours he'd spent lost in online games might finally pay off after all.

Then a tortured metallic shriek came from somewhere near the back of the shuttle, and the display screen flickered and died. Glitch felt a flash of panic. The shuttle jumped upward as though it was a car hitting a bump in the road. A big bump. A warning buzzer burst into life, the sound harsh and grating against Glitch's nerves.

The shuttle gave an enthusiastic lurch, and Glitch was thrown across the cabin. He slammed into the wall and fell to the floor, the impact knocking the wind out of him.

With an almost deafening whine, the shuttle's engines kicked into overdrive and the shuttle began to decelerate. The nose of the shuttle dropped. Glitch grabbed at a metal post jutting from the wall, just managing to stop himself from sliding across the cabin and into the control desk. The sound of the engines died away, then the shuttle hit something. The impact nearly tore Glitch's arms from his sockets.

There was a heavy thump, and the shuttle tipped onto its side. Glitch lost his grip and fell. His ankle twisted as he landed, and a spear of pain shot up his leg. Glitch screamed and collapsed, clutching his ankle.

The shuttle tipped sideways, righting itself and rolling Glitch back onto the floor. He lay there, eyes closed, as the shuttle rocked back and forth, settling after the impact. He felt a jab of pain in his stomach and coughed.

"Are you okay, Glitch?" It was Anderson.

Groaning, Glitch raised an arm and gave a halfhearted

thumbs-up. He was still alive. That was good enough.

There was a loud hissing and a sharp crack. A tear appeared near the control panels. Steam billowed into the cabin. Sparks cracked and popped. Another crack opened, this time in the ceiling that was now the wall, a few feet away from Glitch's head. More steam burst into the shuttle, quickly followed by a steady stream of water.

Anderson called from the back of the shuttle, "We need to get out of here."

Glitch forced himself to his feet and checked his injuries. His arms, legs, and back hurt, and he was pretty sure if he thought about it too long, so would his head. But by some miracle, nothing seemed broken. He clambered through the cabin doorway and joined Anderson and Zheng in the back of the shuttle. Water was streaming in through more cracks in the hull.

Glitch scooped up a handful of the water and splashed it onto his lips. "Saltwater. As long as we didn't bounce too far off course during reentry, we're in the Pacific Ocean."

Doctor Zheng raised her eyebrows but said nothing.

"That'll be a good thing," said Anderson, "assuming we don't drown."

The three of them moved to the shuttle's door, and Glitch pressed his hand against the controls. There was a soft buzzing sound, but the door stayed closed. He slammed his hand against the button four or five times, shouting in frustration.

"We need to find another way," said Anderson.

"A better way," said Glitch. He could almost feel the anger emanating from Zheng.

The shuttle swayed as they moved around, searching for a way out, pressing their hands against panels, twisting and pulling anything that looked as though it might be a door handle. A couple of times, something clunked against the side of the shuttle. Glitch pictured sharks bumping into it as they investigated the strange new arrival to their waters.

The water rose faster and faster as the weight of the shuttle dragged it beneath the sea. Moving around was getting harder. The cold seeped through their clothes and into their bodies as they fought through the water. Soon they were all shivering, teeth chattering. Anderson had grown pale, and her head kept tipping forward as though she was going to pass out. With a burst of sparks, the lights inside the shuttle went out, plunging them into blackness. The water had reached their waists.

Glitch heard the others splashing around, their movements becoming more and more desperate as the water rose. He reached for his flashlight, but it was gone, lost somewhere along the way. Sweeping his arms around to keep his balance, Glitch tried to picture the shuttle, to orient himself and find the most logical place for an emergency exit, but he'd lost all sense of direction. Something brushed against his leg, and he pulled back. He lost his footing, falling backward into the icy waters. He flailed around underwater for a moment then managed to find some traction and push himself upright. He coughed, spitting saltwater and wiping it from his eyes. The shuttle groaned and tipped to one side.

"Move to the high end," called Anderson, spluttering as water lapped into her mouth.

Glitch shuffled forward, his feet catching on the uneven surface. His foot caught on something, the webbing maybe, and he felt a momentary surge of panic until he twisted his foot free. The pain in his stomach was growing, and he pressed his hands against it in a fruitless effort to deaden the sensation.

Distracted and unable to see, Glitch walked straight into someone. They seemed too short to be Anderson. Doctor Zheng, he thought. Picturing the annoyed look on her face, he mumbled an apology.

"It's okay," said Anderson.

Pain sliced through Glitch's stomach as though someone had rammed a rusty screwdriver into his gut. He let out a cry. Water filled his mouth, leaving him spluttering for air. His foot slipped on the slick metal, and he fell backward, beneath the water. He panicked, swallowing more water as he flailed around. He kicked, and the pain intensified, every movement agony. The world around him dimmed.

Glitch felt arms beneath his shoulders pulling him up. His feet found purchase, and he pushed his head out of the water. Coughing and spluttering, he pressed his head against the metal above him. The water rose steadily over his face, and the pain in his stomach grew worse.

CHAPTER TWENTY-THREE
A Watery Grave

As the shuttle plummets toward Earth, Glitch manages to repair the controls, and Kalith shows him how to pilot the craft. Glitch guides the shuttle through Earth's atmosphere while Kalith protects the interior from the worst of the heat. Finally, the shuttle breaks through the atmosphere and crash-lands in the Pacific Ocean. The water rapidly cools the shuttle's hull, and it cracks, letting in water. As Glitch, Zheng, and Anderson search for a way out, the shuttle sinks.

Pain sliced through Glitch's stomach. He felt as though someone had rammed a rusty screwdriver into his gut. He let out a cry. Water filled his mouth, leaving him spluttering for air. His foot slipped on the slick metal, and he fell backward, beneath the water. He panicked, swallowing more water as he flailed around. He kicked, trying to right himself, but the pain intensified. Every movement he made was agony. Dark clouds crept in at the edges of his vision.

Glitch felt arms beneath his shoulders, and someone pulled him upright. Spitting out the water, he pressed his head against the metal surface of the shuttle. The water steadily rose, and the pain in his stomach grew worse.

Water rolled over Glitch's face, flooding his mouth and nose. He shifted position, trying to find one last pocket of air, something to keep him alive for a few seconds longer. Explosions of light burst across his vision, and his head swam. His lungs burned. His face pressed against the metal skin of the shuttle, and it shifted, giving way a little. Hope flared, and he pushed against the ship. The metal resisted then gave way. Light flooded into the shuttle, and Glitch pushed his head out into the fresh air.

He coughed and spluttered, gulping at the air. Zheng appeared beside him. Together, they pushed back more of the shuttle's outer shell until they could clamber out. Glitch dragged himself to the edge of the opening, spitting water. He peered into the shuttle, searching for Anderson, but there was no sign of her. He plunged his hands into the water, sweeping them around, desperately trying to find her.

And then she was there, swimming through the water toward him. She broke the surface and dragged in three long, deep breaths. Glitch and Doctor Zheng helped Anderson drag herself out of the water. The three of them lay on the shuttle, broad grins across their faces. The shuttle rolled slightly, rocked by the waves, but it seemed to have stopped sinking. At least for the time being.

Glitch looked at Anderson. "You going to be okay?"

Anderson nodded and let her eyes drift closed, breathing deeply.

Glitch looked past her, out across the unbroken expanse of the ocean. Off in the distance, he saw three black shapes just above the horizon. As he watched, they grew larger until he could finally work out what they were: helicopters. Glitch lay back against the warm metal. Above him, the sky was clear and blue, and he felt the sun beating down on him, easing the chill from his bones. He smiled.

Pain tore through Glitch's stomach, and he screamed.

CHAPTER TWENTY-FOUR
The Awakening

When Glitch opened his eyes, all he could see was the intense whiteness of the afterlife. It took him a couple of minutes to realize it was just the glare of the fluorescent lighting.

Slowly, he tilted his head to the right. On a battered metal cabinet was a small vase of red and white flowers. He could just detect their smell above the harsh tang of disinfectant. Beyond the table was a broad window, and beyond that was the green expanse of a lawn. In the distance, he saw a nurse pushing someone along a pathway in a wheelchair.

"You're awake."

Glitch turned to face Anderson. She was leaning against the wall on the opposite side of the room. Her thigh was heavily bandaged, and she was leaning on a thick black walking stick.

"Good morning, Captain."

"I thought you were going to call me Scarlett."

"Okay, 'good morning, Scarlett' it is. Nice cane, by the way."

Anderson smiled and walked stiffly across the room to Glitch's bed. "How are you feeling?"

He hesitated. "Actually, I feel pretty good."

"You should, Dwayne," said another voice. Doctor Zheng stood in the doorway. "The government spent a lot of money getting you sorted out."

"Sorted out?"

Anderson reached up to a shelf beside the bed and retrieved a small glass container. She held it up to the light for Glitch to see the red-tinged liquid inside. Something was swimming in it—a worm-like creature about two centimeters long.

"The God's Essence the Barash gave you contained a parasite. Lots of them, actually. Their effect on people varies. For the doctor and me, they just stimulated our taste buds in different ways. For you, they were poisonous."

Glitch instinctively held his stomach.

"Don't worry," said the doctor. "You're in the clear now. They've filtered every last one of them out of your blood."

Glitch looked at the worm writhing in the liquid and shuddered. "Who are 'they'?"

"The government," said Anderson. "You're in a military medical facility near San Francisco. The Air Force picked up the shuttle on radar when it hit the atmosphere, tracked where it landed, and came to get us."

"You're lucky they did," said Doctor Zheng. "We don't know how much longer you'd have lasted."

"What about Kalith and the shuttle?"

Anderson shrugged. "Both gone. Apparently the shuttle sank before the Air Force could secure it. There was no sign of Kalith. Our guess is she had a way to get home."

"And the planet, has NASA found it yet?"

"Yes and no," said Anderson. "It appeared for a while and caused all sorts of excitement. The doctor was right. It affected tides, the weather, everything. And of course the entire planet went Mystero crazy. Every professor and crackpot in the world had a theory about where it came from and what it meant for Earth. There're at least seventeen Churches of Mystero, and those are just the ones we know of."

"Mystero?"

Doctor Zheng grimaced. "It was never officially named."

"There was an Internet poll," said Anderson. "Mystero won."

"So what happened to… Mystero?"

"It vanished again," said Zheng.

"It collapsed?"

"Maybe, but if it did, there's no trace of it. Not that anyone's given up looking."

"Has anyone tried going back through the gateway?"

"The gateway we used has been dead since Smith blew it up," said Anderson. "As far as we know, there aren't any others."

Glitch lay back on the bed, suddenly weary. "At least we stopped Smith. And Kurtz."

"Yes," said Anderson. "Now you get some rest. There're a few people who will want to talk to you, just to get your side of the story. Then, as long as you promise not to talk to anyone about what happened, you can go home."

Glitch nodded and let his eyes drift closed. Home. That sounded like a very good idea. As sleep settled over him, he let out a deep breath and promised himself he wouldn't enter any more competitions. In the future, he'd leave the intergalactic adventures to Buster Crabbe.

About the Author

Philip Harris is a speculative fiction author and video game developer. Originally born near Oxford, England, he now lives on the West Coast of Canada where he spends his days developing video games and his nights writing speculative fiction - anything from horror to science fiction to fantasy.

His first publication, *Letter From a Victim*, appeared in the award winning magazine, *Peeping Tom*, in 1995. Since then he has been published in numerous magazines and anthologies including *Garbled Transmissions, So Long, and Thanks for All The Brains* and James Ward Kirk's *Best of Horror 2013*.

He has also worked as security for Darth Vader.

For up to date information on new releases, free ebooks and other exclusive extras, please sign up to the mailing list at http://solitarybooks.com/upnews.

You can also find his blog and more free fiction at his website.

Website
http://www.SolitaryMindset.com

Twitter
@SolitaryMindset

Facebook
https://www.facebook.com/SolitaryMindset

Goodreads
https://www.goodreads.com/SolitaryMindset

WOULD YOU LIKE SOME FREE BOOKS?

As a thank you to my readers, I'm giving away four ebooks to everyone who signs up for my newsletter.

Just go to the website below for more information.

http://solitarybooks.com/upfree

Did you enjoy Glitch Mitchell and the Unseen Planet?

You can help!

Honest reviews are extremely helpful for all authors and help bring my books to the attention of other readers. Without reviews, books languish unread and unloved, and nobody wants that.

If you enjoyed this book, I would be really grateful if you left a review wherever you bought it, or on Goodreads. It can be short, just a few words on what you enjoyed about the story and why.

Thank You.
Philip Harris

Printed in Poland
by Amazon Fulfillment
Poland Sp. z o.o., Wrocław